T0156561

iUniverse books may be ordered through booksellers or by contacting:

*iUniverse
1663 Liberty Drive
Bloomington, IN 47403
www.iuniverse.com
1-800-Authors (1-800-288-4677)*

*ISBN: 978-1-4401-2281-1 (sc)
ISBN: 978-1-4401-2282-8 (ebook)*

Printed in the United States of America

iUniverse rev. date: 4/1/2009

CHAPTER 1

THE THIRD BODY WAS the straw that broke the camel's back. Not that the first two didn't get some attention, turning up as they did about a week apart on the steps of an old Catholic church in a part of town overrun by tourist traffic. The killer practically had to stand in line like some out-of-towner in order to dump the stiffs. The first one had been stabbed so many times that by the time it was stretched out on the church stairs, it had already bled out. This saved the padres a tough clean-up job and a tougher public relations problem. They weren't so lucky with the second cadaver. It showed up a week later with most of the back of the head surgically removed by gunshots and planted face down for the maximum dramatic effect on passersby. Both these murders were gruesome enough, but at least within the realm of possible violence in any major urban center. The third one was another story entirely. It showed up ten days after number two, on the same church steps with his hands in his front pockets. This doesn't sound too bad, except that his arms were tied to his ankles behind his back. He'd also had his eyes gouged out and they were found in his hands, in the pockets. The feeling was that he'd been strangled, but it was hard to say because his throat had been cut as well. A dollop of dog shit had been stuffed in his mouth for good measure. Sometimes the small touches make all the difference.

The three cadavers had something else in common besides their final resting place. All of them had whip marks covering their backs.

This type of urban littering generally puts a crimp in the local tourist trade. By the time the third body appeared, the area merchants, already somewhat antsy in light of their thinning tourist clientele, started making their displeasure known at the highest levels. This led to a spate of superficial activity that consisted of a loud press conference by the police commissioner and a flurry of articles detailing police progress on the case. This was followed by an increasing lack of interest as the murders receded from the present to the preterit to the past perfect tense. A couple of weeks went by and no new bodies appeared, so the general public went back to focusing on this month's rent and groceries. The victims had never appeared on anybody's society page and were considered working class, if they had been working at all. They were also black, at least by New York standards, even though their skin colors ranged all the way from Halle Berry to Don Cheadle. Of course, the hometown press described them more accurately, calling only the first victim a black man, while the other two were referred to as mulattos.

That's the kind of distinction people make in the city of Salvador, state of Bahia, in Brazil.

I was blissfully ignorant of all this action since the police blotter of Salvador almost never gets printed next to the sports pages of The New York Post. Plus, my attention in the month of April rarely ventures south of Houston Street, focused as I am on my own rent and groceries. I manage to cover those expenses by tending bar at the world famous White Horse Tavern of Greenwich Village, in between private detective jobs for Mike Breza Associates, where I am both Mike Breza and the associates all rolled into one.

Early one Tuesday morning after a late shift at the bar, I came home and found the message light on my answering machine insisting that someone had called. I ignored it and went to bed, only to be awakened at the ungodly hour of eight a.m. by a ringing telephone. Seconds later ghosts of cases past came drifting out of the receiver.

"Alo? Mike Breza?"

"Yeah, I think so. Who's this?"

"Oy, Mike, you don't recognize my voice?"

With less than five hours sleep, I could barely recognize my own bedroom.

"Uh, no, I'm sorry. Who is this?"

"Mike, it is Anjo Denovo from Brazil."

Now that was a name I could recognize. A year and a half earlier Anjo Denovo had come to New York and helped me solve the murder of my older brother's Brazilian girlfriend, Isabela Alvim. I had gotten stomped, punched, shot at and chewed out in the process, but in the end Anjo and I had managed to find the killer. Along the way Anjo had saved my life, stolen my would-be girlfriend and taught me more than I had ever wanted to know about the Afro-Brazilian religion of Candomble. He'd also done penance for his sins by introducing me to a Brazilian woman who subsequently became my girlfriend, although I'm not sure that's how Anjo had planned it. She had recently pulled up stakes to return to Rio de Janeiro, but not before I'd taken a number of lessons in Brazilian culture and Portuguese.

"Anjo Denovo? I can't believe it! It's great to hear your voice. How are you doing and why are you calling me so damn early in the morning?"

"Oy, Mike, it is not so early, eh? It is nine o'clock in the morning here in Salvador."

"Yeah, well that's still pretty early for me. What can I do for you, man?"

There was a moment of silence on the other end of the call, an unusual occurrence for a man as loquacious as Anjo.

"Mike, I need your help."

"Talk to me, my friend."

And talk he did. It seemed that all three of the murder victims that had wound up on the steps of the church in Salvador had belonged to Anjo's ceremonial place, called a terreiro, in Salvador. He described the grisly circumstances to me and judging by his frequent pauses and labored breathing during the narration, I gathered that he knew all the victims pretty well. A tired sigh told me he'd reached the end of what he had to say. Now it was up to me to ask some questions.

"Anjo, let me start by saying I'm very sorry for the loss of your three friends. I'm sure it's very difficult for you. But I have to ask you, why me? This sounds like a case that would be much better handled by the local police. What value can I add?"

"Mike, the local police, as you say, have already investigated the case and in spite of telling everyone that they continue to investigate, they are not doing anything. The last body appeared a month ago and everybody forgot everything related to the case during Carnival at the end of February. Now it is like the murders never happened."

"Anj, I'm not trying to contradict you here, but maybe the case is tougher than it seems on the surface and maybe the cops really are trying to investigate without any luck. Isn't that a possibility?"

This time the sigh I heard was borne more of exasperation than fatigue.

"Mike, I know my country and I know very well the police here in Salvador. If the victims had been rich, the city would be building additional jail cells to hold the suspects being dragged in for questioning. These men were not rich, they were poor, even by the standards of Northeast Brazil. They were poor and they were men of color, so the police don't give a fuck about them. That is why I need your help."

I was gratified to hear that Anjo hadn't forgotten all the important New York vocabulary I had worked so hard to teach him.

"Okay, so what do we do?"

"I need you to come to Brazil, to Salvador to help me solve these murders."

I wasn't sure if I liked the idea or not. Visiting Brazil sounded cool, but sticking my nose into an ongoing police investigation didn't sound too smart to me in any language. So naturally I accepted.

"I don't know what my problem is, Anjo, but I'll do it if I can get the time off from work and if I can manage the finances. When would you like me to come down?"

"Tomorrow would be good."

"Jesus, what ever happened to the world famous laid back Brazilian attitude of 'whenever is fine'?"

"In this case, Mike, I think I lost it when the third member of my terreiro appeared dead on the church steps."

It was hard to argue with that.

CHAPTER 2

AFTER I HUNG UP with Anjo, I thought about going back to bed, but a hot shower and breakfast seemed like a better idea. I was toweling myself off when the phone rang again.

This time it was a more familiar voice, my older brother, Jim.

"Hey, Mikey how are ya?"

My theory was that older brothers were incapable of letting go of childhood nicknames because it would force them to recognize that their younger siblings had left them far behind on the growth chart. I was always going to be five feet tall for my brother and he was going to call me "Mikey" until the first spade of dirt hit my box.

"What's up, Jimmy? You hit the wrong button on your speed dial?"

"No, because I don't have you on my speed dial, since it's reserved for people who can actually help me. I had to dial you manually, pal, and my index finger is killing me."

"Well, don't overdo it with all that exercise. What can I do for you?"

"Nothing. I hear you're going to Brazil."

"Your ears need cleaning because I've got a couple of major league "ifs" blocking my way."

"Yeah, yeah, yeah, I know, time off from work and finances. I just hung up with Anjo Denovo and he told me the whole story. You and I both know that time off from the White Horse is no problem, so that just leaves finances as your big "if". Am I right?"

"Yes, but you and I also know that for the branch of the Breza family that isn't a partner at a major New York law firm and in fact scrapes by serving frosty recreational beverages to parched clients, finances are an eternal "if"."

"Well, I'm calling to change that "if" to a "when"."

"Come again?"

"I'll pay for your trip to Brazil. Plane ticket, hotel, food, drinks, you name it, I'll pick up the tab."

"That's mighty generous of you, James."

"Not really. It's the least I can do for Anjo after all the help he gave you in solving Isabela's murder."

"Well, I just hope I can give him the same kind of help."

"Mikey, there's nobody better than you at this detective stuff and if anybody can help Anjo, it's you."

My other theory about younger brothers was that they were incapable of letting go of the thrill they felt when their older siblings paid them a compliment. The corollary to the theory was that the younger brother could never let it show.

"Do you need me to insist that you shouldn't do it before accepting?"

"Nah, we both know you're going, so just help Anjo find the psycho who's killing his people."

"I'll do my best. And thanks for the vote of confidence."

"You just be careful, Mikey. I'll have my secretary contact you to make all the arrangements and send you the tickets."

I pulled on some clothes while I pondered my good fortune. A free trip to Brazil sounded like a nice vacation. If I played my cards right, I might even have some fun while I worked with Anjo. Maybe I'd even be able to avoid getting my ass kicked like I did the last time I worked with him.

I decided to save the nostalgia for some other time and went downstairs to get some breakfast. Halfway down the elevator shaft I picked up the scent of my doorman's cigar. Sure enough, when I stepped into the lobby, there was Jimmy Keane, former middleweight boxer from Hell's Kitchen, at his post pulling on his first smoke of the day.

"Big Mike. You're up early today."

"Morning, Jimmy. Guess who I heard from this morning?"

"I dunno, your brother?"

"Well, him too, yeah, but I was thinking about my first phone call of the day. You remember my buddy, Anjo?"

"Are you kidding me? My arm still hurts me when I think about it."

Jimmy had taken a bullet in the arm as a result of the case Anjo and I had worked on together in New York. It turned out to be the shot heard around Manhattan as every second generation Irish member of the NYPD top brass took a personal interest in seeing that the shooter got his.

"Yeah, well it looks like I might be going to Brazil to help him out."

Jimmy peered at me through his morning puffs.

"You're gonna do some detective work down in Brazil?"

"Looks that way."

Jimmy nodded his head and gave me the same advice I'd gotten from him for the last ten years.

"Just keep your left up, Mike, just keep your left up."

After a quick breakfast at the Village Den with my favorite dining companion, The New York Post, I arrived back at my apartment to find a very detailed message from my brother's secretary. She had researched times and dates of flights, addresses of hotels, what kind of clothes to wear and even what level of sunblock I was supposed to use to maximize protection, but still look like I'd been out of town for a couple of days. The menu of options was a little overwhelming to listen to, let alone memorize, before eleven o'clock in the morning, so I called her back and had her reserve a flight for Salvador for Friday. That gave me a couple of days to avoid packing my bag so I could do it at the last minute, thereby forgetting important toiletry items that would surely not be available in the third world. I was thirty-four years old and there was no point in starting to make things easier for myself at this stage of the game.

CHAPTER 3

BY THE LOOK ON her face, the lady at the Varig airline counter on Friday had never seen a five year old passport that had never been opened. She stared at my Brazil visa like she thought the ink was still drying. I asked her to be gentle since it was my first time.

It wasn't really my first time on an airplane, but nobody was likely to confuse me with Charles Lindbergh, either. I'd taken trips here and there in the United States, once even out to California in my younger days, always in coach class. So I didn't think anything about making the flight to Brazil under the same conditions. And the truth was that the first five hours were nothing I hadn't experienced before. It was the last four hours when I discovered that too much exposure to canned air results in the aerial equivalent of road rage. When even Brazilians, easily the most outgoing, friendly people I had ever associated with in New York, started complaining loudly and getting snippy at the stewardesses toward the end of the overnight flight, it meant the world wasn't getting as small as everyone said it was. The spontaneous applause that erupted when the plane touched down in Rio had nothing to do with the pilot's performance. It was anticipation of fresh air on the part of the passengers.

I had to change planes in Rio and with an hour and a half to kill, I had no problem making it to the connecting gate. I even stopped for a small cup of Brazilian coffee, called a cafezinho, on the way. I'd been drinking cafezinhos in New York on a semi-regular basis since working with Anjo and I thought I was prepared for the real thing. It was just the latest in an ongoing series of misconceptions I had developed about the real world. The high octane caffeine content with just the right amount of too much sugar didn't quite convince me that I could just run the nine hundred plus miles north to Salvador, but I was damn well ready to pedal the plane if they needed me.

It was a smooth two hour flight, my cafezinho stomach turbulence aside, and I stepped into the 2 de Julho International Airport at about eleven-thirty a.m. local time. Since my luggage consisted of a decent-sized backpack, I breezed through customs and waded into the throngs of Brazilians waiting for loved ones and computer parts at the exit. I had just reached the shallow end of the mob when I heard the voice I was listening for.

"Oy, Mike Breza, aqui, cara, aqui."

I turned to my left and damned if Anjo Denovo wasn't walking toward me, waving his arms and showing me a grin that Magic Johnson, the Mona Lisa and the Cheshire Cat couldn't collectively piece together on their best day. Then I heard another voice call my name.

"Hey, Mike, Mike Breza. Over here!"

I looked to my right and thought I was seeing a mirage. It was my cousin, Gary "Bones" Renfrow, six feet of tan and goatee, walking my way, waving his arms.

They both hit me with a hug at the same time, figured out there was a pair of arms too many, stepped back and looked at each other. My bronze cousin was on one side and my dark-as-they-come Brazilian host on the other.

I heard "Hey, who's this guy?" in stereo, so I made the proper introductions.

"Anjo, this is my cousin, Gary Renfrow. Bones, this is my friend, Anjo Denovo. Gary, Anjo lives here in Salvador. Anjo, I don't know what the hell my cousin Gary is doing in Brazil."

There, I'd done my part. Anjo then threw his arms around Gary and gave him the classic Brazilian greeting hug.

"If you are Mike Breza's cousin, you are my friend, too, Gary."

"The pleasure is all mine, Anjo. O prazer e meu."

"You speak Portuguese?"

"A little bit. Enough to get by."

Anjo looked at him with approval, giving me a chance to speak up.

"So, Bones, the last I knew, you were living the good life in St. Petersburg, Florida. What brings you to Brazil?"

"Mike, you really have to talk more with your family. Or maybe less, I'm not sure which."

Gary's mom was my mom's kid sister and she was the cool aunt of the family, which meant that when I was a kid, she loved to do all the things that my own parents didn't. Of course, if they had, I would've been mortified. Gary had inherited the coolness gene and had made a career out of turning backwater vacant lots all over the state of Florida into attractive franchise sites for some hotel chain, all without putting anything more formal than flip-flops on his feet. His fifteen year run had come to an end a few months ago as the market slumped and the Sunshine State finally ran out of room for new hotels. The hotel chain cut him loose with a severance package worthy of Bill Gates, so he headed for the golf course with his wife and daughter. After a month or so, he bought a new sailboat and decided to try it out. The girls stayed home while he sailed through the Caribbean and south, winding up in Salvador about ten days before my arrival. His crew had flown back to the U.S. and he was just about to head north again with a local crew when the family grapevine told him I was coming, so he made it his business to meet me at the airport.

"So brother Jim gave you all the details?"

"Well, actually his secretary did, but it's the thought that counts."

"So where's your boat?"

"It's down in the lower city, by the Modelo Market."

That didn't tell me a whole lot, but Anjo let out a low whistle.

"You have a veleiro in the harbor by the Mercado Modelo? Which one is it?"

"The white one at the end of the dock."

"It must be a beautiful boat."

"Well, it got me here and I'm hoping it gets me back. You want to stay on board with me, Mike? It'll save you the cost of a hotel."

The one sailboat experience of my life had ended with me painting the deck with an expensive lunch out in New York harbor. Somehow the idea of having a boat as my home base in Salvador didn't particularly appeal to me.

"Bones, I'm going to pass on the offer, but thanks just the same."

"Can I at least get you to come take a look at it? How about you, Anjo?"

Anjo's enthusiasm was only matched by my reticence.

"I would very much like to see your boat."

"Great. Let's do it in the next couple of days because I'm taking off for home as soon as Mike finishes…What are you doing here, Mike?"

I looked over at Anjo and he nodded, giving me the green light to tell.

"I'm here to help Anjo try to get some information on a couple of murders."

"Whoa! Sounds heavy and I won't ask for more details, but you know that if I can help in any way, all you have to do is ask."

"Fair enough. How about telling me where I can get a taxi into town?"

Anjo held up his hand."

"Senhores, do not worry. Follow me. I have arranged everything."

Five minutes later, after strolling through a parking lot in stifling ninety degree heat, I was sitting in the front seat of an official tourist taxi from Salvador with Anjo at the wheel and Bones in the back. I knew it was an official tourist taxi because the handwritten placard taped above the glove compartment said so. The car itself was some kind of Volkswagen model that wasn't sold in the United States, most likely because the car had somehow made it out of the factory without seatbelts. Bones didn't seem too worried about it, but he was seated a long way from the windshield. I wasn't sure if Anjo knew what a seatbelt was, but from the way he drove, it looked like the information might prove useful someday. At least he didn't have the meter going.

"Anjo, where did you get this taxi?"

"It is mine, Mike. It is all mine."

"Yours? I thought you were a tourist bus driver."

"I used to be a tourist bus driver. Now, after saving my money for years, I am a tourist taxi driver."

He looked over at me and grinned like a man sitting on top of the world.

Chapter 4

As we pulled away from the parking lot, the crisscrossing roads and sidewalks gave way to a single four-lane road that cut through an enormous flat green field. Every several hundred yards or so, an orange jumpsuit stood out against the deep green background as a maintenance worker stabbed at stray papers or other trash trying to flee the premises. We passed through some sort of gate in a chain link fence that obviously marked the boundary of the airport and turned left on to a divided highway, where in less than a mile it became evident that we weren't in Kansas anymore. That was where we saw the first of a series of houses made out of what looked to be rotted boards, corrugated tin and cardboard. Even with my lack of geometry skills I could see that none of the walls formed anything resembling a right angle. The buildings leaned toward one another like drunks on a bender and none of them looked like they had any floor other than the dirt below them. Clotheslines with light-colored garments were strung wherever it looked like their tension wouldn't pull the wall down and there were little kids, barefoot and minimally dressed, playing among a varied menagerie of animals; chickens, goats, donkeys, horses, all of them dressed at least as well as the kids. There were some adults moving around the houses and an occasional vehicle parked in what looked like its last resting place. Finally, there was trash, lots of it, although it was mostly concentrated in piles that looked as controlled as a trash pile can be. Anjo caught me staring out the window.

"Oy, Mike Breza, welcome to the real Brazil."

"Anjo, is this one of those slums, uh, favelas, you once told me about in New York? With drug gangs and all that?"

"No, Mike, the favelas are part of the city of Salvador. This is just a place where very poor people live."

Bones piped up.

"It doesn't look like much of a life."

"It can be very difficult here, but it is even worse in the favelas."

"How so, Anjo?"

"Guns and drugs, Gary, too many guns and drugs."

The three of us shut up for a bit and we passed a few more settlements at regular intervals along the highway. Then the landscape started to acquire a more urban flavor with factories, gas stations and warehouses streaming by. We passed through some kind of roundabout and between a couple of parks before hitting the Avenida Otavio Mangabeira. Before I knew it, the stereotypical Brazil of beautiful beaches appeared on my left complete with exotic names like Garden of Allah and Artists' Beach. I was hoping Anjo would turn off at any moment to take us to his beach house, but he just kept driving and the landscape got progressively less beachy and more urban. By the time we passed a zoo and a huge shopping center to reach some lighthouse, I had given up any hope of working on my tan from Anjo's back deck. He stayed on the main drag, which for a while was called Seventh of September Avenue before changing names a couple of times and suddenly we were at a series of docks at the end of which a huge white sailboat dwarfed everything else in the water. It had "Sweet St. Pete" painted on the back and there were about five or six of the skinniest, black would-be sailors ever to swab a deck leaning against posts or sitting on boxes in the vicinity of the boat.

"Holy shit, Bones! Is that your sailboat?"

"Sure is, Cuz. What do you think?"

"I think I'm going to move to Florida and start selling hotel franchises!"

Anjo could only whistle.

"It is a very beautiful sailboat, Gary."

Bones hopped out of the back seat and stretched.

"What hotel are you staying at, Mike?"

I fumbled in my backpack for the all-important piece of paper with all my travel info.

"Looks like the Hotel do Chile."

"That up near the elevator, Anjo?"

"Yes, on Rua Chile. Chile Street. Number seven, next to the Praça de Castro Alves."

"I'll meet you guys up there in about forty-five minutes, okay? I've got to check on the boat and pay my protection money."

I couldn't believe my ears.

"Bones, those guys there are watching the boat? The living stickmen? Man, you're lucky they're not just watching it sail away. How are those guys going to stop anybody? They don't weigh two hundred pounds between them."

Bones grinned at me and I noticed Anjo was doing the same.

"Anjo, do you want to tell him or should I?"

Anjo wagged his index finger at Bones, giving him the green light.

"They might look skinny, Cuz, but those are some hard men. They fell out of the womb and landed on these docks. If only half of the stories I've heard them tell are true, it's amazing that they're still around to tell them. This is their turf and nobody in this town will fuck with these guys. Trust me."

Normally I wouldn't trust a real estate salesman from Florida, but the glint from the sun hitting the business end of an enormous knife one of the security crew was using to peel a mango lent some credence to his story. Bones was all smiles and backslaps as he waded into the posse and they all looked happy to see him. Anjo looked over at me.

"Your cousin has met the right people on the docks if he wants to sleep well at night."

"Yeah, well, my cousin has always had the knack for meeting the right people and getting along with them."

"And you, Mike?"

"Anj, you know I'm just the opposite. First I meet the wrong people, then I piss them off. And I've got the scars to prove it."

He reached over and put his hand on my shoulder.

"Thank you for coming down, Mike."

"Anj, it's my pleasure, but don't thank me yet. I still haven't done anything and there's a whole city of wrong people out there just waiting for me to piss them off."

He laughed.

"I am sure you won't disappoint them."

He started the engine and we headed to the hotel.

CHAPTER 5

WE DOUBLED BACK THE way we'd come, drove up a street steep enough to play varsity in San Francisco and somehow made it onto the Rua Chile. Then Anjo pulled over in front of the whitest building I'd ever seen. It couldn't have been more than six or seven stories high and a small sign over the entrance barely whispered Hotel do Chile. I got the impression that anybody who'd ever been on the beaten path didn't stay there. Anjo spoke with somebody on the sidewalk that addressed him by name and made the universal flip of the hand to tell him it was all right to leave the car there. I grabbed my minimal luggage and followed Anjo in the door.

The lobby was as bright as any room I'd ever seen and it was all sunlight streaming in from the window on my right as I stepped in. The sunlight reflected off the white walls, lighting up the narrow entrance that opened slightly to accommodate a check-in counter on the right. Beyond the counter, the room widened even more into a waiting area complete with a sofa, a throw rug, a coffee table and a couple of chairs. A stairway going up was on the left hand side, opposite the sofa, and an elevator was hidden behind the stairs. Beyond the sofa was the entrance to some kind of small dining room.

I was just starting to sweat over the prospect of speaking my broken Portuguese to the check-in guy behind the counter, when Anjo smiled and held up my key. He then introduced me to João.

"Mike, this is João. This is his hotel"

I shook his hand and stammered out some Portuguese.

"Mooeetoo prahzer, João."

"Hey, your Portuguese is very good."

The weight of the world, or at least South America, suddenly lifted from my shoulders.

"Not as good as your English, João."

"Well, I lived in New York for a few years. In Astoria."

Astoria, Queens was home to South Americans of all stripes and had the best Latin American restaurants in all New York City.

"I probably shouldn't be surprised by that, but I am anyway. It's nice to meet you, João, in any language."

"If you need anything while you stay here, you just ask for me. Any friend of Anjo is welcome here."

"Will do, man. Thanks. Obrigado."

Anjo and I walked back toward the elevator.

"Christ, Anjo, you're like the mayor around here. Between you and my cousin, I'll know all the important people in Salvador in no time."

My room was on the fourth floor, back toward the front of the building and faced west toward the bay far below. I tossed my pack on the bed, took a leak and was ready to go.

"Okay, Anjo, let's get to work. Where do we start?"

"How about downstairs waiting for your cousin?"

"You're the boss, my friend."

When we got downstairs, we found Bones chatting up João in what seemed to me to be a mixture of broken Portuguese, reconstructed Spanish and wobbly English, none of which impeded the conversation. They shook hands like brothers when we stepped out the door and João gave me a big thumbs up. Out on the street Anjo opened his trunk and pulled out some kind of backpack before leading us down the Rua Chile. The buildings were the most amazing structures I'd ever seen and they got more spectacular with every block. Most were two to four stories high and topped off by sloping roofs covered with red tiles that looked almost handmade. White was the most popular façade color, but there were all kinds of pastel colors as well. Buildings were painted powder blue, lime green, cinnamon red, puffball pink, to the point where I thought I had wandered into a game of Candyland. The doorways were at least ten feet high and the few doors I managed to glance inside of led into rooms with ceilings at least that high. The narrow sidewalks in front of the buildings were so neat that even Martha Stewart would have declared them a good thing. I shot a look at Bones and was happy to see that he was gawking as well. At least I wasn't the only blatantly obvious tourist in the group.

We made a couple of turns and crossed a couple of cobblestone streets that reminded me of the far West Village in New York City before we finally stopped at an open air cafeteria on some kind of plaza. Anjo said it was the Praça da Se. We sat down at a table towards the inside, away from the plaza and were immediately set upon by a kid wearing some kind of light blue waiter's smock who looked too young to be working legally anywhere in the Americas. Anjo whispered something to him and before I knew it, three cold bottles of Brahma beer were standing at attention on the round table. There was also a laminated, hand-written menu in case we wanted something more solid.

"Anjo, what's the specialty of the house?"

"I always have the cheese sandwich when I come here."

"What do you think, Bones?"

"Who am I to argue with the culinary authority?"

"Okay, Anjo, get us a bunch of cheese sandwiches."

He raised an eyebrow and the underage smock was all over him and then gone. While I took a sip of my Brahma, Anjo lifted his backpack onto his lap, pulling out a stack of newspapers. He unfolded the one on top and placed it in front of me. The screaming headline said DEAD!!! in Portuguese, but it was the picture that almost made me choke on my beer. It was a full color close-up of the second corpse left on the church steps that took up the entire front page below the fold, leaving nothing to the imagination. He was a muscular man with cinnamon colored skin, laying on some stone steps with his arms extended in front of him like he was diving into the afterlife. I could see the gray matter that was still inside his skull and the whipmarks on his back were practically wet to the touch. A large cheese sandwich had appeared beside me, but I suddenly had no appetite for it. I looked over at Anjo and saw his mouth set in a hard line. Bones was looking down at his sandals. Anjo sighed.

"His name was Flavio Guimarães."

I nodded.

"He was a friend of yours?"

Anjo grimaced.

"A friend, a companion in my terreiro, a filho de Shango, a good man."

Something in the photo caught my eye and I leaned closer to the paper to have a better look. There were some particularly gruesome marks at the base of his back and they were unmistakable.

"Hey, Anjo, there's a swastika carved into his back. Did you see that?"

Anjo and Bones leaned over to see the paper, but I didn't need their confirmation.

"Anjo, do you have photos of the other victims in that stack of papers?"

He started rummaging around and handed me a couple more papers. The first one wore the eye-catching phrase KILLED AT CHURCH!! with a photo just slightly smaller than life size. It was of the first victim, a dark black man who had been stabbed to death. He was lying face down, but still had on what had probably been a white shirt when the mayhem had started. It had ridden halfway up his torso, but the photo had been taken from too far away to make out any details. The second paper announced NUMBER THREE!! at full volume and had a photo worthy of National Geographic in its clarity and detail. It was taken from an angle above the hog-tied cadaver and right there in the center of the victim's lower back, surrounded by whipmarks, was a small swastika. I practically knocked over my beer when I jumped to my feet.

"Got it! There it is!"

Anjo leaned over again, but Bones barely lifted his eyes before studying his footwear again.

"Anjo, do you have any better pictures of the second cadaver? I'd like to see a close-up of his back if you've got it."

He started digging through his pile of tabloids, but I couldn't wait so I grabbed half and started sifting through them myself. I found two pictures of the cadaver I was looking for, but both were too small. I also found photos of battered wives, abandoned kids, drunken men and half-naked women. Man, this paper had it all! Anjo tossed me something from his pile.

"Mike, is this a better picture?"

It was. So was the one next to it. The photographer must have been the Brazilian Weegee, a real crime photo artist. The first photo showed the cadaver's face, right down to its dirty tongue, but the other photo was the one I wanted to see. It was another shot from above the victim that fit the entire body in the frame without sacrificing any detail. The exposed lower back was very clear and peeking out from under the boxer shorts, which had also ridden up somewhat, was something that looked like half a swastika, hidden among the furrows made by the whip. I pushed it across the table to Anjo.

"Anjo, can you see a swastika peeking out from under his shorts?"

He took a hard look and nodded his head.

"Yes it looks like the top part of one."

I was about to congratulate myself on what a great detective I was, but I was interrupted by a sonic gagging that came from the men's room behind Anjo. It was then that I realized Bones was nowhere to be seen. Another thundering retching sound followed by an equally loud "Oh, God!" confirmed where he was and what he was doing. Then it was the sound of water swirling south, more water being splashed around and suddenly Bones reappeared in the land of the living, a little green around the gills, but definitely still breathing. He sat back down at the table and, hard-living seadog that he was, took a big gulp from his beer. He looked at the two of us and shrugged his shoulders.

"Sorry, guys, I'm not real good with the sight of blood."

"Don't sweat it, Bones, I'm not so good with the sight of the ocean. Especially with a boat deck beneath my feet. Anjo, did the cops come up with anything on the swastikas?"

He shrugged.

"I have not heard anything or read any articles in the paper about the swastikas."

That would've struck me as odd on my home turf, but what the hell did I know about Brazilian cops, robbers and reporters? I tore off a piece of newspaper and stole Anjo's pen to make a note of asking the cops about the swastikas. Then I grabbed my fair share of the cheese sandwiches before my cousin with the now-empty stomach could finish them off. As I was looking under the plates for stray crumbs, Anjo suggested we take a walk to see more of the center of the city. I told him I was game, but that I wasn't going anywhere without a couple more cheese sandwiches. He gave me a broad smile.

"Oy, Mike, if you like the cheese sandwiches, wait until you try some real Bahia cooking."

"Just promise me it'll be as good as the Cabanha Carioca in New York.'

He looked offended.

"Mike, por favor, do not compare the real Bahia food with the stuff prepared by Mexicans in New York."

"Hey, Anjo, I'm ready to be educated, but right now all I care about is getting my cheese sandwiches. Man, I didn't realize how hungry I was."

I slapped both of their hands away from the arriving plate and defended my nourishment tooth and nail. Mostly tooth.

CHAPTER 6

I LEFT THE RESTAURANT with a sense of accomplishment, although I wasn't sure if it was because of the swastika discovery or the sandwiches. Anjo took us to the far side of the Praça da Se, past some kind of fallen cross statue, past a cathedral that made St. Patrick's look like plain vanilla, through a courtyard named, naturally, after Jesus, and past a couple of other churches whose names didn't so much escape me as not penetrate my consciousness, seeing as how there seemed to be one every other block. I was also a little preoccupied with not letting my mouth hang open as I continued to gape at the architecture. Anjo led us on a downward sloping path through narrow streets that had been built with the word "quaint" in mind and I noticed that the farther we walked, the more people seemed to know Anjo. He was nodding at every third person he passed and if he didn't nod, he was tossing off two or three words of greeting. We passed a sign announcing the house of some guy named Jorge Amado on our right before Anjo stopped in a small, irregularly-shaped plaza. He turned and smiled back at Bones and me.

"Here we are. O Largo do Pelourinho. This is the people's center of Salvador da Bahia de Todos Os Santos. Here is where Brazilian life really started in the sixteenth century."

It must have been quite a beginning. Cobblestone streets wriggled off in every direction with promises of ever-increasing charm around every bend. They were so narrow I felt like I could reach into the windows on both sides of the street at once. The sky was a deep blue with the sun straining to bleach out the pastel rainbow of the buildings from the second story up. The lower levels were drenched in shadow and the contrast between light and dark made everything seem cooler, even if the thermometer disagreed. All of the buildings pre-dated the French and Indian War and were still housing people, stores, businesses and more. Suddenly the two hundred twenty-odd year history of the United States didn't seem like such a long time. Anjo snapped me out of my deep thoughts.

"You know what means "Pelourinho", Mike?"

I shook my head.

"How about you, Gary?"

The same reaction.

"I hope my English is strong enough to pronounce the word correctly. It means pillory."

"Pillory?"

"Yes, did I say it right?"

"Beats me, I'm not real familiar with the word. Bones, you?"

"Yeah, I think it's a place where they used to punish criminals in public by locking their head and hands in some kind of board or something."

"You mean like stocks?"

"Something like that. Does that sound right, Anjo?"

He looked a little puzzled.

"I am not so sure what are these stocks you are talking about, but the pelourinho was also a place to punish criminals and slaves."

I wasn't sure I really wanted to know, but I asked anyway.

"What was the punishment, Anjo?"

It turned out that the "pelourinho" was a stone column that stood in the middle of the plaza with some kind of bronze ring attached to it. The designated bad guys, some petty criminals, but mostly rebellious or recaptured slaves, had their arms tied to the ring and were then publicly whipped in a classic example of torture as spectator sport. The Largo do Pelourinho wasn't the original site of the Brazilian whipping post. It had bounced around a bit in search of the perfect site. One of the previous placements had been the plaza we had already passed through, where the cathedral stood. However, it seems that the shrieks of pain from the victims used to disturb the concentration of the Jesuits in the cathedral during their important religious ceremonies and, as a result, the pillory was moved down to its final resting place right in front of us. The ruling elite gradually came around to the idea that public floggings were in bad taste, so the column eventually passed from the scene, but not without first giving the neighborhood its catchy name. I felt better knowing there was a seamy historical underbelly to the visual charms of the neighborhood. It went well with the newspaper photos we'd seen. When Anjo finished his explanation, he started walking toward the far end of the plaza.

"Where to now, Anjo?"

He motioned for Bones and me to follow, as if we had any choice in the matter, so we fell in after him. We started walking on Carmo Hill, made a quick left onto some Gomes Street, before making a right onto Do Passo Street. Same stunning architecture as before, except that now my general travel fatigue was starting to immunize me against it. Then, about a quarter mile down Do Passo Street we came upon a church that even a jaded, jet-lagged New Yorker like me could tell had been something special. It looked a little run down, but anything built in 1737 was bound to show a little wear and tear. It had twin bell towers that must have launched into the sky like bleached rockets before the white paint had chipped off. They framed a small dark cross that stood out for its simplicity when compared with the ornate trim on the towers. There were five windows across the façade that were subdivided into maybe forty smaller panes of glass, all with a narrow white trim that was the bane of some poor window washer's existence. The brightness of the white window panes contrasted nicely with the worn brown stone that threatened to overtake what little remained of the original paint job The entrance consisted of three arched wooden doors set inside carved wooden frames that rivaled the trim on the towers for attention to detail. The huge doors were closed, but looked like a team of horses would be needed to open them at Mass time. Across the narrow street in front of the church, enclosed by a black, cast iron fence, a broad cement staircase tumbled downward, broken into three or four different landings, abruptly ending at another black, cast iron gate and fence on the sidewalk of the street below. The view of the church from down there must have been even more impressive, with the towers and cross set off against the tropical blue background. Even Bones, Protestant background and all, was impressed. He elbowed me.

"That, my friend, is one beautiful church."

Anjo looked at us looking up at the towers.

"It is a spectacular church and has been so since 1737. It is the Igreja do Santissimo Sacramento da Rua do Passo."

Bones made a slight change in his analysis.

"That, my friend, is one beautiful, old church."

Anjo's sigh, heavy enough to knock down the main door, made me realize the reason for the guided tour.

"Anj, I'm guessing this is the church where the three victims woke up dead."

His nod was heavier than his sigh.

"They weren't up here by the door, right? They were down on this huge stairway leading up here to Do Passo Street."

Anjo's nod was slightly less heavy.

"Exactly where on the steps were they?"

He pointed toward the bottom.

"They were all the way down by the fence, about halfway between the bottom and the first terrace."

"Can we get down there for a closer look?"

"Yes, but we must go around to the Ladeira do Carmo."

We doubled back on our original path and swung around on Carmo Hill to reach the bottom of the stairway that led up to the church. The iron fence was about six feet high and each vertical bar had an unfriendly point at the top, making it a very unattractive fence to scale. There were also no horizontal bars to plant your feet on except for the two that ran across the fence at about foot five of the six foot height. I looked through the bars and counted about ten steps up from sidewalk level to the first landing. There was also a four or five foot sidewalk separating the inside of the fence from the stairs. I looked over at Anjo and he had his arms folded, resting his chin in his right hand. He looked lost in thought, but I had a few of my own to clarify.

"Hey, Anjo, you said the bodies were about halfway up the stairs from here to the first landing?"

He nodded.

"That's about five steps up from the sidewalk, right?"

Same nod.

"Who's got the keys to this gate?"

He couldn't get away with only moving his head this time.

"Only the priests of the church of the Santissimo Sacramento. They open the gates before Mass and close them after."

"Are you sure they're the only ones with keys?"

"I am pretty sure. Why?"

"Well, judging from what we're looking at here, the folks who put those bodies on these steps either had a key to open the gate or some kind of crane to hoist them over these urban harpoons that make up the fence. Call me crazy, but I'm guessing that a crane operating around here in the wee hours of the morning would probably attract some attention. Any ideas?"

Anjo stared at the steps for a couple of seconds before breaking into a broad grin.

"No, but this is why I am only a taxi driver and you are a great detective. You are already thinking of things that no one here in Salvador has mentioned."

I wasn't feeing like such a great detective at that moment. I was feeling more like a jet-lagged bag of mush. The beer and the cheese sandwiches weren't helping much either, not to mention the heat. The shady part of the sidewalk was starting to look like a great place to stretch out for a couple of hours, so I knew it was time to head back to the Hotel do Chile.

"Anjo, can you get me back to the hotel? I'm starting to run out of gas."

"Oy, Mike, what you need is a bom cafezinho."

Tired and wired didn't sound like the way to go my first day in Brazil.

"I'll pass on the offer, Anj. I think I need to stretch out, study the inside of my eyelids and try to absorb what I've seen since I got here. Bones, you all right with that?"

"Yeah, I've seen enough bloody pictures and beautiful churches for one day."

Anjo smiled.

"Now all you need to see are some beautiful women."

Bones shook his head.

"Don't even talk like that to me. I've been away from my wife for too long."

We wound our way back up Carmo Hill, Alfredo De Brito Street, back past the churches and our cheese sandwich shop. All the colonial architecture that had fascinated me on the way down had now somehow morphed into a technicolor blur on the far side of my fatigue. The only building I cared about was the Hotel do Chile and when we got there, it was all I could do to slap hands with my cousin and defend myself against Anjo's embrace.

"Mike, you look very tired. I will let you rest tonight. Let's have breakfast tomorrow and we can talk about how we want to work."

"Sounds good to me, Anj. What time?"

"I will pick you up at nine o'clock."

"Great. Bones, what about you?"

"I've got some stuff to do on the boat. If you feel up to it, come on down later. I'll be there."

I nodded at him and we split up. João was nice enough to get me my key with a minimum of conversation and once upstairs it only took me two tries to get it to work in the lock. I don't even know if I did anything else before falling face down on the bed.

CHAPTER 7

THE WET SPOT ON my pillow finally woke me up a couple of hours later and I had to look around the room for a couple of seconds before I could figure out why my furniture looked so different. There was only the faintest light drifting in the west-facing window and my watch said six o'clock, which meant that it was seven o'clock wherever I was in Brazil. I shuffled over to the window and saw the lights of the city just starting to come together as the horizon faded to black over the bay. Yeah, it was Salvador, that's where I was and I had brought my hunger with me. I went into the bathroom, splashed my face and headed out in search of food.

There was a lot more movement on Rua Chile than I had seen during the day and I had to bob and weave for a few steps when I got out of the hotel. I remembered that Bones had invited me down to the boat and I also seemed to remember that most large sailboats prone to being on the high seas for weeks at a time usually carried food with them. Even if I was wrong, Gary still had to know more about where to eat in Salvador than I did. I was walking up the street trying to figure out how to get down to the docks with the minimum damage to my knees, when I came upon what looked to be the Municipal Plaza of Salvador. My first clue was a building that advertised itself as a Camara Municipal, my second was an even bigger palace with a huge white dome in the center that would have given the U.S. Capitol Building some serious decoration envy. There was also a huge elevator at the western end. I remembered that Bones had mentioned something about my hotel being close to an elevator, so I walked over to check it out. Even with my weak Portuguese, I could figure out that this particular elevator was named Lacerda and that it probably didn't go up from where I was standing. I tried to blend in with all the locals when the doors yawned open again and followed the crowd in. I made a real friend with the operator since I didn't have any local coins and was forced to give him a dollar. His smile and nod told me it was a very good tip and I nodded back at him. The flow carried me out to the lower part of the city on Conceição da Praia Street. I could see the docks stretching out in front of me and I took more or less the shortest route I could to get there.

Bones was sitting on the deck of the Sweet St. Pete with a beer, watching the daylight slip away. The guardians we'd seen earlier in the day were nowhere to be found. I decided to get nautical on him.

"Ahoy, matey!"

He turned around leisurely in his chair and even in the growing darkness I could see the scorn on his face.

"Did you just say 'ahoy, matey' to me?"

"Aye, aye, sir!"

He rolled his eyes.

"Okay, Popeye, I'm gonna let that slide here in Brazil, where nobody understands it, but if you ever talk that way to me in the States, it'll take a lot more than a can of spinach to save your ass. Come on aboard."

I strolled up the ramp and plopped down in the chair next to him. He offered me a Brahma beer from a small cooler parked at his side.

"I'll only accept your beer if you can tell me where to get something to eat. I'm starving."

With that, I accepted the beer. Bones tooted on his beer bottle like a whistle. I took it to mean he was thinking.

"The bad news is that the supplies I've got below are some of the worst eating anywhere on the seven seas."

"And the good news?"

"The good news is that we're not on the seven seas and there are a couple of restaurants just up the street in the market. Problem is they're kind of expensive, relatively speaking, that is."

"Well, as long as they've got something besides cheese sandwiches, I'm okay with that."

"You won't regret it, Cuz."

He stowed the bottles below and we stepped down to the dock. Bones stuck his right thumb and middle finger into his mouth and let rip an eardrum-puncturing whistle that was so loud I half-expected a New York cab to show up. Instead we got one of the skinny guys I'd seen that afternoon. Bones said a few words to him in Portuguese and the guy gave him the thumbs up with a big gap-toothed grin. Bones patted him on the shoulder and we started walking back toward the Lacerda Elevator.

It took me no more than a couple of blocks to learn that even the darkness of night oozed charm in Salvador. We entered a plaza called Praça Cayru and went into a big yellow building called the Modelo Market. It looked like a warehouse of tourist shops, but up on the second floor there were two restaurants sharing the same patio. One was called Camafeu de Oxossi and the other Maria de São Pedro. While it looked like they even shared the same door, they sure as hell had different hostesses. These were two large, striking women and they were dressed to the nines. They were both decked out from head-wrap to sandals in clothes that were so white they belonged in a detergent commercial, while the deep ebony of their skin made them seem even whiter. The dresses were made of layers of ornate lace and they seemed to envelope the women without actually touching their skin. They sported several necklaces of varying lengths that fell to different levels of two attention-getting chests and they had hoop earrings the size of which had never been seen outside of Washington Heights in Manhattan. As soon as they saw us heading for the entrances, they both started waving and telling us to come in their particular restaurant, which was much better than the dump on the other side. At least that's what I imagined they were saying, since my Portuguese wasn't strong enough to provide for an exact translation. But being from New York City, I knew a hard sell when I saw it. We stopped at the top of the stairs, mere steps from the well-dressed, gesticulating women. I looked at Bones.

"Well, where do we eat?"

Instead of the eenie-meenie I was expecting, he immediately walked left to Camafeu de Oxossi.

"I ate in the other place last night."

The losing hostess was shaking her head like we were making a huge mistake until Bones leaned over and explained that he'd eaten in her place the night before. She brightened up a little, but nothing like the hostess who hooked us. She escorted us in past a small bar that was obviously there to get client stomachs lubricated for maximum food intake while they waited for their tables. Past the bar, she handed us off to some inside staff with high volume compliments about how smart we were to choose her restaurant. Just as she was about to turn away, I risked some of my Portuguese and asked her name. She said something that sounded like "Vahnda Meerahnda" and I butchered a "thank you" in Portuguese. She gave me a big smile and went outside to hustle up some more customers.

The room was round and enormous, with fifteen foot ceilings. Both the floor and ceiling were made of dark wood, giving the impression of being in some kind of palace. That impression was reinforced by the bright white walls and the view of the bay that burst in through the huge open windows. The place was sparsely populated at best, so the waiter got us seated with beers and a menu in record time. Mine was in English, so I knew my performance with Vahnda Meerahnda hadn't gone unnoticed. Bones had already put his down, so I figured he was going to be my culinary guide for the night.

"Okay, Mr. Bahia food expert, what do I order here?"

"Well, you've only got two choices for your first real meal in Bahia."

"And those choices are?"

"You either get the vatapa or a moqueca. It doesn't get any more Bahian than that."

"The vah-tah-pah or the moe-kay-ka? Which is which and what makes it so?"

"I could try and walk you through it, but the back of the menu does an infinitely better job."

As near as I could make out, a vatapa was fish, shrimp, onions, tomatoes, coconut milk, dende oil and some kind of cream sauce seasoned with cashews, almonds and spices that I didn't recognize, even in English. A moqueca was a kind of fish or shellfish soup that had lemon, tomatoes, onions and other ingredients that started to make me dizzy. I chose the vatapa because I liked the way the word sounded. Also because it was the first thing on the menu.

"Okay, Bones, what are you up for?"

"I'm getting the lobster moqueca because I had the vatapa next door last night."

Our waiter took our order in flawless English and we sipped a couple of Brahmas while we waited. The main dining room looked out over the bay and over to the left we could see where the Sweet St. Pete was docked. The décor was late twentieth century weathered wood and the room seemed kind of empty for a Saturday night. I estimated thirty tables and only seven were occupied. Maybe Bahia wasn't the party town I had imagined. I decided to consult my expert.

"So where is everybody, Bones? The joint ain't exactly jumping."

He glanced at this watch.

"Mike, it's only eight o'clock. People in this town haven't even woken up from their naps yet. Wait until ten o'clock and it'll be standing room only until one in the morning."

My faith in Anjo's town was restored by my cousin's analysis and then reconfirmed when the food arrived. My first thought was that the reason I hadn't recognized the spices in the menu's description of the vatapa was that they were probably used in New York only to melt ice on the sidewalks in the winter. But after the third bite I either got used to it or had lost all ability to detect temperature on my tongue. At any rate, it ceased bothering me and the rest of the meal was one of the top culinary experiences of my life, although I did need three beers to keep the fire down to a two alarm level. Neither Bones nor I said a word for about fifteen minutes, limiting our communication to loud grunts of satisfaction. By the time we stopped chewing, there wasn't much more than pieces of shell and cartilage on our plates. We focused on breathing for a few minutes after that before finally giving up on dessert.

"No coffee for you, Bones?"

He shook his head.

"Nah, I need to sleep tonight. You?"

"I think I'll start my day tomorrow with a cafezinho instead of extending my night with one now."

The settling of the bill consisted of me protesting weakly as my more successful cousin slapped a wad of local currency on the table. I looked around the room as I stood up and as Bones had predicted, it was packed. Most of the patrons seemed to be tourists, but it looked like a pretty good local scene as well. The small bar by the entrance was serving rivers of beer and wine and the bartender was holding his own in a very cramped space. A not insignificant number of the future diners were very attractive women and I wondered if it might be worth my while to skip breakfast and lunch every day so I could afford to eat there a couple more nights during my stay.

Out on the street, the city had come to life. People were everywhere walking, talking, drinking, laughing and music seemed to seep out of every doorway. I told Bones about the breakfast date with Anjo at nine and he said he'd meet me at the hotel. He headed back to his boat and I drifted back toward the Lacerda Elevator. The streets were packed, the women were gorgeous and a few even looked back at me. Some of them might have been working, but I didn't want to spoil my ego trip my first night in Salvador, so I ignored that salient fact all the way back to the hotel. Then I got back to work drooling on my pillow.

CHAPTER 8

EIGHT AND A HALF solid hours later there was way too much sunlight seeping in my window. My eyes opened in spite of my brain's protests about it being only six in the morning for the rest of my body. A normal shower did me no good at all, so I stepped back in and left out the hot water this time. My manhood went from tenor to soprano in nothing flat and the cobwebs went south from my head to meet it. A nice cafezinho would get me ready to take on the streets of Salvador once more. I threw my clothes on, grabbed a backpack with a notebook, and went downstairs.

It was still too early for either Anjo or Bones to be in the lobby, so I stepped out the front door after giving João a top o' the morning nod. It was a quiet Sunday morning on Chile Street. The pristine blue sky looked like it had infinite potential, so I started walking. I followed the only path I knew, the one back towards the Lacerda Elevator. The first sign of human life was a small, slow-moving group in the elevator square. They were sporting some serious finery, but I couldn't tell if it was their Saturday night or Sunday morning best. Not even their yawns gave me a clue.

I hung a right across from the elevator on Tira Chapeu Street and walked up to Ajuda Street where I finally saw someone obviously on the front end of her day. It was a black woman dressed in all white like the hostesses from the restaurants the night before. Two steps later I realized it was the same woman who had ushered Bones and me inside the restaurant Camafeu de Oxossi. Her outfit was a little less ornate than the night before, but there was no mistaking the blazing white of her theme. She had her back to me and was setting up a small table with what looked like cakes or pastries. Since it was early I was still feeling bold, so I tried out my New York Portuguese on her.

"Bong gee-ah, Vahnda Meerahnda."

She wheeled around to see who could be the owner of such awful pronunciation. It took only a fraction of a second for the surprise in her eyes to give way to a broad smile and even less time for my boldness to evaporate once she started to speak. It took her three or four sentences to recognize my silence for the terrified incomprehension it was. When she did, she slipped easily into a broken English that made my Portuguese sound even worse.

"No speak Portuguese too good?"

I shook my head.

"No, I'm still learning."

Her smile bucked up my courage.

"Ah-eendah eeshtoh ahprendendoo."

She threw her head back and laughed.

"Hey, you pretty good for Portuguese. What your name?"

I held out my hand and she took it in hers.

"Mike Breza."

"Breza? You know what means Breza in Portuguese?"

"Not really."

"It means small, cool wind."

"Oh, you mean a breeze?"

"That's it, Mike Breza. From where you come?"

"New York City."

"You here for tourist?"

"Nah, I'm here to help out a Brazilian friend of mine."

"What his name?'

"Anjo. Anjo Denovo. Do you know him?"

She spread her arms wide and tipped her head back in the international symbol for "Come on, how am I not going to know Anjo Denovo?" She then spun around and grabbed three or four of her cakes and shoved them at me.

"Friend of Anjo? You take these. No pay! No money!"

I stepped back without touching her merchandise.

"I'll only take them if you let me pay."

She wagged her index finger and made a "tsutsutsu" sound at me through pursed lips.

"You here to help Anjo, you don't pay!"

She produced a bag, stuffed the pastries inside and forced them into my hands. Without letting go of my arm she whispered in my ear.

"Anjo my babalorixa, He is very good man. You help him and you good man, too, Mike Breza."

She stepped back to her table of pastries and extended her hand again to give me a card. It said "Wanda Miranda – Doces e Guloseimas" with a phone number. I stuck it in my pocket, but I was still embarrassed to be taking a street vendor's merchandise without paying.

"Look, Wanda, are you sure I can't pay you for these pastries?"

All I got was a second round of "tsutsutsu".

"You help Anjo, that is my money."

At that point some other people on the front end of their day stopped in front of Wanda's pastry table. Since they looked like paying customers, I figured my protests were at an end. I decided to try a thank-you in Portuguese.

"Okay, Wanda, moo-eetoo ohbrigadoo."

Her smile stood out once more against the perfect ebony of her skin as she worked her table.

"Okay, Mike Breza, bom dia para voce."

I heard some church bells start to ring and realized it was nine o'clock. Even more importantly, it was breakfast time, so I stuffed half a pastry in my mouth as I got to Chile Street. It had a caramelized sugar coating with some kind of sweet filling inside that made me want to skip breakfast and go back to buy Wanda's entire inventory. I was still licking my fingers when I stepped in the hotel entrance. Bones and Anjo looked right at home leaning against the front desk, sipping a cafezinho and chatting with João. I made their morning by slipping them each one of Wanda's pastries. With one bite, Bones' eyes were rolling back in his head while Anjo and João were grinning from ear to ear. Anjo nodded at me.

"You met Wanda Miranda?"

"Yeah and she wouldn't let me pay when she found out I was a friend of yours."

He shook his head.

"Wanda is a good friend of mine. She belongs to my terreiro and knew the three victims very well. She is also the best person to get advice from in all of Salvador. She is also a very powerful mãe de santo."

"That means she has some pull with the orixas, right? Like you with Shango?"

Anjo nodded.

"She is very strong with Ossaim, the healer."

Bones was licking his fingers as he spoke.

"Well, she's got the best pastries, that's for damn sure."

Nobody argued and we left for some real breakfast.

CHAPTER 9

ANJO TOOK US TO some place that wasn't much different from where we had eaten lunch the day before. Everybody in the place knew Anjo and most of them came by to greet him. This put him a long way behind Bones and me in shoveling eggs with buttered toast and black beans into our gullets. I even ate a banana to get some variety in my diet. When the well-wishers faded to none, Anjo finally ate and talked while Bones and I sipped our cafezinhos.

"Oy, Mike, I hope you had the opportunity to rest last night."

"A solid eight hours. Maybe more."

"That is good. What do you consider the next step in the investigation?"

Normally I hated getting hard questions so early in the morning, but at this point the ultra-sweet coffee had both of my working brain cells in overdrive.

"I think the next step is to talk to people that knew the victims well. Their families, their friends, that sort of thing. Maybe they can help us piece together where the victims were the nights of their deaths, if anybody was pissed off at them or if they were wrapped up in anything shady."

Anjo had a quizzical look in his eye.

"What means shady?"

"You know, something illegal like drugs or some other criminal activity."

"I do not believe these men were criminals."

"Anj, you're probably right, but I'd still like to hear it from some other sources, if you don't mind. I need to get a little more background on all three bodies. I guess we can start with asking if they knew each other."

Anjo shook his head.

"They all belonged to my terreiro and they probably saw each other at the ceremonies, but I don't think they were close friends."

"Sounds good. Let's see if we can get the families to confirm that."

"This would be a very good time because the football games do not start until two o'clock."

Bones leaned over and whispered in my ear.

"That would be soccer for all you uncultured Americans visiting Salvador."

We took Anjo's cab to visit the second victim's family. It wasn't that far, but apparently you couldn't get there by public transportation on a Sunday morning. We drove a few miles north along the bay to Boa Viagem Beach and parked the cab at a very uncrowded taxi stand. We then hiked in from the water, following a street with no discernible name up a hill dotted with all kinds of structures from corrugated tin shacks to cinderblock forts. Every one of them looked ready to slide downhill to bayside as soon as the next sprinkling of rain hit the ground. The house we stopped at was an amalgam of wood, tin, bricks and plastic sheets covering the windows. Anjo rapped on the lopsided door, calling out a woman's name.

"Dona Eva!"

There was the sound of bare feet shuffling on a dirt floor and the door creaked open, pushed by a caramel-skinned boy of about four. His eyes were a delicate shade of green and the ringlets on his head were tending toward blond. Right behind him was a woman who broke into a smile as the child called her Mom and told her who it was at the door.

"Dona Eva!"

"Dom Anjo!"

They hugged each other and exchanged double cheek kisses before Anjo introduced us. Dona Eva was just as effusive with Bones and me and practically pulled us into her home. She was coffee-colored, wearing a clean, short, denim skirt with a red t-shirt. Her head was covered by nascent dreadlocks that rose up and peeked out over a wide yellow headband.

I was taken aback by how neat and organized the inside looked. It was one large room with two or three straight-back metal chairs arranged around a solid wooden dining table that supported a remarkably large color TV against the wall opposite the door. A couple of light bulbs were strung on exposed wire in a haphazard fashion across the ceiling. One dangled off to the deep left over a humming refrigerator and the other looked ready to torch the sofa next to us that was aimed at the

TV. Over to the right were a couple of hammocks and a twin bed. The floor was a reddish dirt that was harder and smoother than any linoleum floor I had ever passed out on.

Anjo explained the reason for our visit and Dona Eva nodded as she went back to the refrigerator to grab three Cokes. She insisted the three of us sit on the sofa while she shooed her son, whose name sounded like Marcelo, outside to play. Anjo looked at me as she pulled one of the metal chairs in front of the sofa.

"I have explained to Dona Eva that you are here to help us obtain justice for her husband, Flavio."

"That's the second victim, right? Flavio Guimarães?"

Anjo nodded and Dona Eva did the same when she heard her husband's name.

"What are the questions you need to ask her?"

"Can she tell you and can you tell me where Flavio was supposed to be the night before his body turned up on the church steps?"

Anjo translated into Portuguese and I pulled out my notebook. It turned out that Flavio was out for a night of revelry with the boys and wasn't supposed to go much farther than a couple of local bars. He had a regular posse that he hooked up with, mostly guys he'd known all his life, played soccer with, etc. He went out with them at about nine o'clock on a Saturday night and Dona Eva went to bed before he showed up, something that happened from time to time when the drinks were flowing among friends. Marcelo woke her up early the next day asking for his dad, but it wasn't until about nine a.m. that Dona Eva started to worry. She went out looking for him and his drinking buddies, to a man, said they had split up at around two-thirty in the morning. She checked every single tavern where he'd ever been known to have a drink, but nobody had seen Flavio Guimarães after two-thirty.

"Okay, so where was he when the group split up at two-thirty?"

"She says the group separated in front of the bar at the foot of the hill."

"What hill? The one we just climbed? There's a bar down there?"

I was a little disappointed I hadn't noticed it. We bartenders are supposed to be aware of the competition. It was called Amor Cego or Blind Love. I jotted down the name thinking that Blind Drunk was probably a better description if the group had started tanking up at nine p.m.

"Can Dona Eva think of anyone that might've wanted to hurt Flavio? Somebody that he might've pissed off or owed money to or something? Any enemies?"

Dona Eva shook her locks at me.

"Did he have any dealings that were illegal, like drugs or anything like that?"

Another head shake. Unless we came up with something from the Amor Cego or his drinking buddies, I didn't see us making a lot of progress. I looked up from my notes and stretched out my best optimistic smile.

"That's really about it, Anjo. Please tell her that if she thinks of anything else that might be important to let us know."

"What will be our next step?"

"We should try to talk with Flavio's buddies and maybe check in at the bar down the hill. Oh, and if she can tell us what detective she talked with, maybe we'll try to get some help from him."

Dona Eva listened to Anjo's translation, but just gave him a puzzled look.

"Mike, she says she never spoke with any detective or anybody else from the police."

CHAPTER 10

I WAITED UNTIL WE were about twenty yards from Dona Eva's house before I asked the obvious question.

"Anjo, how is it that the cops never talked to Dona Eva about the murder? How'd she find out what happened?"

Anjo pursed his lips and took a deep breath.

"Mike, this is how things work here in Salvador. The death of a poor mulatto is not the type of crime the police are paid to solve. They are busy solving crimes committed against wealthier, more important people. I think Dona Eva found out from the newspapers or the television that Flavio's body had been found near the church."

It wasn't the first time I'd run into an economically selective justice system, but I'd never seen one quite so blatant. I'd also never expected to see it in Brazil, which has the reputation of a racial paradise compared to the U.S.

We were just about at the end of the path leading back to the taxi stand when I saw the hand-scrawled sign for the Amor Cego on the left. I jerked my head towards the door and Anjo led the way. The door was unlocked and somehow stayed on the hinges as we passed through into a big rectangular room. The wooden walls looked slightly sturdier than popsicle sticks held together with Elmer's glue, but not much. A long bar fenced in by a few stools faced us, unlike the bartender who sized us up in a Brahma beer mirror that hung over the cardboard cash box behind the bar. The earlybird patrons sprinkled among the five or six tables did the same. We must've passed inspection because nobody left and no firearms were produced. Anjo chatted up the barkeep and ordered three beers, which came out nice and cold. They were a nice balance to the caffeine-and-sugar water we'd just sucked down. Anjo turned to Bones and me.

"Jorge says he remembers Flavio and his friends being here the night he disappeared. He confirms that they left just as he was closing at almost two-thirty."

"Did he see them leave?"

Anjo made a quick consultation.

"He says they all went out the front door except for Flavio, who went to the bathroom first."

That was an idea whose time had come. I asked for directions and Jorge pointed at a door to his right in the wall behind the bar. The plumbing I expected to see when I stepped through the door was nowhere in sight, mostly because I was standing in an open lot. Straight ahead about fifteen yards was some kind of outhouse. Inside was a hole whose depth was a mystery, but whose contents weren't. I did my business in record time, holding my breath until I got out. As I was walking back toward the bar, I noticed something in the tall grass to my right. It was an upside down sneaker discarded near a flimsy wooden fence that marked the boundary of the empty lot and separated it from a small ditch with a wide dirt path right behind it. The other sneaker was in the ditch and one of the rails from the fence was holding it in place. I stepped a little closer. There was a narrow furrow leading up to the place where the first sneaker lay, like the foot inside it had tried to dig it into the ground to keep from going somewhere. I let it lay and looked at the sneaker under the fence rail. The white back of its heel was stained the color of the wooden rail. I couldn't make out any other tracks, but it looked to me like somebody had been dragged over the fence. It was worth checking out.

I stuck my head inside the bar and waved Anjo and Bones outside even though they were on their second beer. I pointed out to Anjo what I had found.

"Anjo, how long ago did Flavio turn up dead?"

"It was a little more than two weeks ago."

It didn't seem possible, but I had to be sure.

"Anj, can you go get Dona Eva and ask her to come down here?"

"Of course, but why?"

"I want to see if she can identify these sneakers."

His eyes got wide and he was off like a shot. Five minutes later he and Dona Eva ran out the bar's back door. She came over to look at the footwear. I didn't have to ask any questions. Her tears told me all I had to know. Anjo put his arm around her and led her back into the bar. Bones moved over next to me.

"Shit, Cuz, I'm impressed. How'd you know those were Flavio's shoes?"

"I didn't know, but they looked funny to me the way they were just lying there."

I pointed out the grassless furrow leading up to the closest discarded sneaker and the ghost of another one etched in the ground parallel to the first. Bones shook his head.

"Now that you point it out I can see it, but I wouldn't have seen it before."

He punched me in the shoulder just hard enough to let me know how impressed he was.

"Man, you're a real pro."

We walked back into the bar, where Anjo was serving Dona Eva some hundred proof nerve tonic at a table near the front door. Dona Eva said something to Anjo, who turned to face me.

"She wants to know if you can tell her what happened the night Flavio disappeared."

I shrugged my shoulders.

"Just that it looks like whoever was wearing those sneakers was dragged out of the backyard against his will."

At that point I just shut my mouth. She knew the rest better than all of us.

CHAPTER 11

ANJO WALKED DONA EVA back up to her shack while Bones and I made short work of our beers. When he got back, we walked to the taxi stand to flag a real taxi for Bones so he could get back to do some work on his boat. Anjo and I went back uphill to talk with a couple of Flavio's sidekicks from his last night on earth. Neither Jose nor Edson could give us any new information and their stories couldn't have sounded more alike if they'd practiced them. The only difference was that both claimed to have been the most sober of the group when they'd split up at last call. I'd heard that story before.

We had to get back in Anjo's sled to visit the family of the first victim, a day laborer named Carlos de Souza. He'd hung his hat a little farther up the coast at Monte Serrat Beach and the drill was the same as with the previous address. We parked at another sparsely populated taxi stand and hiked in from the main road up a series of hills dotted with more improvised homes. We took a couple of turns off the main footpath until we came to a shed that was just barely winning the battle with gravity. Anjo called out instead of knocking and from the looks of the place, it was a good decision. It was made of fifty percent sticks, forty percent corrugated tin and ten percent unrealistic optimism. The second time Anjo called out, the blue canvas door flapped opened and a beautiful ebony woman stuck her head out. She looked at Anjo and then stared at me staring at her before asking what we wanted. Even with my weak Portuguese, I understood that Anjo asked for Maria. The woman lifted the rest of the flap and let us in.

There were two women inside and it was a star and a half at best compared to Dona Eva's four-star shack back at Boa Viagem beach. It was smaller, darker and contained much less furniture. Two wooden chairs, a crippled table and a bed were illuminated by a single forty watt bulb connected to some exposed wire running back to its electricity source, which was nowhere to be seen. There was a cooler instead of a fridge in the corner and one of the chairs was occupied by a television set. The woman who opened the door-flap was seated in the other chair while another very dark-skinned woman was on the bed. When she saw Anjo, she whispered his name and started sobbing. Anjo put his arms around her and held her for a bit while I looked for someplace to park my eyes. While they were wandering, they crossed paths with those of the doorwoman. I gave her my howyoudoin' half-smile-and-slight-nod combination and she stared at me like I was some kind of weird science experiment. I let my eyes wander a little more until Anjo introduced me. The words "detective" and "New York" caught my ear and I hoped he wasn't exaggerating my resume. I shook Maria's hand and did the same with the doorwoman, whose name was Teresa Cardoso and turned out to be Maria's sister who lived close by. The change in her attitude was made clear by her haste to rise and offer me the chair. I scored a huge linguistic victory by telling her she could stay seated in Portuguese and moved a little closer to Maria to take notes. With Anjo translating for both of us, I asked Maria for the story of Carlos de Souza's last night.

Carlos had been playing some pick-up soccer down on the beach on a Saturday evening with a group of players that usually showed up at six-thirty or so. Attendance varied, so some of the players were his buddies and some were just local beach players. The games usually went on until dark and sometimes beyond. Afterwards some of the guys might grab a beer, but it wasn't normally a late night. When midnight rolled around and Carlos still wasn't home, Maria had started to worry. She went out looking for him, but came up empty. When she woke up at six the next morning, there was still no sign of him. She went to check with his best friend, a Paulo Amado who sometimes played in the beach pick-up games. He hadn't played the night before and had no idea of where Carlos could have gone. She went shack to shack to see if anybody knew anything, but none of his friends or acquaintances had laid eyes on him. She was in a panic that turned into a state of shock when the afternoon tabloid found its way into the neighborhood. The front-page photo, which I had seen, was easily identified as Carlos. My first question was pretty basic.

"Anjo, can you ask her what the cops said about the case?"

He hesitated for a second, but asked her the question. Her answer was a shake of the head and a few whispered syllables. Anjo looked at me.

"Mike, the police never spoke to Maria."

My crackerjack detective instincts led me to see a pattern developing. A dead body would appear, followed by no cops and no investigation. I looked back at Anjo.

"Nice system you got in this town."

Anjo shook his head.

"Just in this part of town, Mike. The poor part."

I ran her through the litany of questions about Carlos' buddies, contacts and activites. There were no unsavory characters in his life and he wasn't involved in anything illegal. Retelling the story was too much for her and she started to cry. Carlos' body was tossed into some public grave without Maria being able to put together any funeral, although she at least had the opportunity to identify the body in person. I asked if there was anybody else we could talk to about the night Carlos disappeared, but she was sobbing too steadily to answer. She buried her head in Anjo's shoulders so I decided to give them a little space. I nodded at Teresa on my way out. It felt like she stared at me until the flap blocked her vision.

I was glad to be outside. The sun was burning bright, so I decided to stretch my legs a bit while waiting on Anjo. I headed uphill a ways, then hung a left. I hadn't gone more than a hundred yards when I passed the last human structure. A group of kids dressed in blue soccer jerseys on the other side of the path were coming toward me. There must have been about seven, all ready to root for their team. They slowly crossed over to my side and surrounded me. I suddenly remembered why it was always a bad idea to wander around by yourself in a neighborhood you knew nothing about.

Their baby faces said thirteen years old, but the knives and sharpened metal rods in their hands said full-grown thugs. I listened to the weapons. Rule number one when you're outmanned and outgunned is to give the muggers what they want without pissing them off. As always, the leader of the pack was also the shortest guy in the group. He was about five feet four inches tall with copper colored skin and green eyes. Judging from the complete lack of hair on his face and legs, puberty was only a rumor for this kid. It didn't stop him from putting a blade just below my chin as he yelled at me. I didn't understand all the words he used, but his main point was on the end of the knife. I made for my pocket and he grabbed my hand to stop me. One of his taller buddies then reached into my front pocket and pulled out my wad of twenty-five reais. By New York City rules of engagement, that should've been everybody's signal to haul ass out of there, but I was in Salvador, Brazil. One of the kids tugged at my backpack. I jerked it away and managed to stammer in Portuguese that they couldn't have it. I couldn't afford to lose my notes from the morning's interviews. While I was complimenting myself on my Berlitz phrasing, a light flashed in my head and I knew one of the kids had bashed me in the head with a rock. Experience had long ago taught me that the first blood was the hardest to draw. After that it always got progressively easier until you had a feeding frenzy on your hands. Since I wasn't at the top of this particular food chain, I had to do something. I was already dizzy so I started spinning like a top while yelling at the top of my lungs. The kids didn't look like they'd expected a psychotic reaction like this and froze for a second. That was just enough time for me to smack two of them in the face as I spun. I kicked another out of my way as I broke into a run back where I had come from. When I reached the turn that would take me back to shack city, Teresa, the grieving woman's sister, appeared in front of me. Her eyes went from my head to the blue shirts closing in on us. The seven kids saw her and immediately scattered in different directions. All except for one, who froze when Teresa screamed.

"Josue!"

He stood stock still, except for his trembling effort to will himself invisible. He was about five-seven with smooth dark skin and a minimalist afro. Teresa made use of that afro by yanking it so hard I thought she was going to carry him off like a six-pack. I think he might've said something, but I couldn't hear his voice over the litany of Portuguese profanities thundering from Teresa's mouth. She slapped his downcast face two or three times. Then he lifted his head and I saw that he had the exact same face as Teresa. This meant that while her son was blessed enough to share in the good family looks, the downside was that he had to follow his mother's rules. And follow he did, as his mom walked back down toward Maria's house without letting go of the poor kid's hair, screaming in his ear the whole time. I enjoyed the show, although it probably wasn't quite worth the twenty-five reais and blood I'd paid for it.

Anjo and Maria were in front of the blue canvas door when we arrived. Maria's eyes bugged out of her head when she saw the blood trickling down past my ear. She must've figured out the play pretty quickly because she didn't hesitate to start in on her nephew, just like his mom. Two or three slaps later, Anjo moved over next to me to look at the cut on my head.

"Mike, what happened?"

"This guy and his buddies showed me a little favela hospitality. It cost me about twenty-five reais."

"We will get it back, but first we have to clean your head."

"I don't care about the money, Anj, but the cut cleaning would be helpful."

We stepped back into Maria's shanty and Anjo found a plastic bottle of water next to the cooler. It looked cleaner than the mix of blood, sweat and grime running down my cheek, so we decided to use it. He grabbed a rag that was hanging on a metal basin, wet it and listened to me shriek like a magpie when he pressed it against my temple. The fire went out quickly, so I held the rag against my head. Maria, Teresa and her son came in to line up in front of us. The kid had his hands behind his back, studying something very intensely on the floor. His mom and his aunt were on either side of him, waiting with absolutely no patience left on their meters. In a barely audible voice the kid apologized for what had happened. When he finished, his mom gave him an audible slap on the back of the head. This apparently jogged his memory because he went on to say that he'd get my money back. Anjo then added his two cents in a nicely authoritative, mellifluous voice that was equal parts understanding and threat. It sounded like he underscored the importance of getting the money back to its rightful owner and that he, Anjo, would personally hold the kid accountable for it. It was a solid, fear-inspiring little sermon, but there wasn't a snowball's chance in hell of me seeing those bills again and we all knew it. Or at least I did. Hell, I was just happy that my bleeding had stopped.

Once Teresa and Maria slapped Josue out of the shack, they both practically prostrated themselves before me to ask forgiveness. I told them everything was okay and not to worry in my fractured Portuguese. With that, Anjo and I started walking back toward the taxi. He looked over at me and grinned.

"The favelas here in Brazil are different from New York, no?'

I looked at the red stain on the rag I was holding against my head before answering.

"Yeah, well, I seem to acquire head wounds in both whenever I'm with you, so maybe they're not so different. What's our plan now?"

He thought for a second.

"I do not think it is worth the effort to go talk with the third victim's family now. The football games have started and not even grief can overcome football here in Brazil."

"Nothing like the thrill of victory to make you forget your woes."

CHAPTER 12

THE TAXI STAND LOOKED more rumor than real when we got there, Anjo's taxi being the only one in sight. Anjo told me it was unlikely any taxis would appear until late afternoon when the soccer games would be over. I like a town that has its priorities straight. We climbed into the Anjmobile and rode down the coast. He turned the radio on to listen to the game.

The ride back was fast since the streets were deserted. Before I knew it, we were walking along Chile Street after parking the taxi. We passed a newspaper stand on the corner of Das Vassouras Street and Chile Street when some guy called out Anjo's name. He was about five foot ten with skin somewhere between brown and black and a shaved head. As always seemed to happen with Anjo, they embraced like they were long lost brothers. I gathered that the guy was making Anjo some kind of offer, but Anjo was wasn't biting. The guy then looked at me and asked Anjo who I was. He broke into a grin wider than Fifth Avenue and motioned for me to come over. He threw his arm around my shoulder and I understood that he was thrilled to meet a friend of Anjo's from Nova Yorkee. He apparently had a great opportunity for me as well. I looked at Anjo.

"Anjo, what's the play here?"

He scratched the back of his head.

"My friend Nelson is offering both of us a bee-shoe for half-price today."

"That might be more interesting to me if I knew what the hell a bee-shoe was."

Nelson was looking back and forth between us like a sale was imminent. Anjo was looking like he didn't really want to give the necessary explanation, but didn't know how to avoid it.

"A bee-shoe is a word for animal here in Brazil. Nelson is a cambista for the jogo do bicho here in Salvador."

Nelson started to nod real fast when Anjo said "jogo do bicho".

"I'm still not with you, Anj."

"It is a gambling game where you bet on an animal and if that animal is chosen, you can win money."

"Oh, okay, it's a government lottery."

"No, it is not run by the government."

"Then who runs it, some charity?"

"Mike, the jogo do bicho is a private operation that is run by an organization that makes its living with the jogo."

"So it's a private lottery?"

He nodded.

"Is it legal?"

He scrunched his face up.

"Not exactly, but it is tolerated. And it is a national hobby. Everybody plays the jogo do bicho. It is an enormous business in Brazil and everybody knows about it. Most big cities have their own operation and thousands of people make their living off the game. There are three drawings every day and different kinds of bets can win different amounts."

So it was an illegal lottery that everybody in the country knew about and played. It also looked like a hard sell approach in public, much like the one our buddy Nelson was giving us, didn't attract any negative repercussions. My first guess was that payoffs to the right people had to be involved. That was the gist of my second and third guesses as well. While I'd never been to Rome, I had heard the expression about how to act when there. If everybody played, I was game for a try.

"Okay, Anj, so how do we play?"

It turned out that there were twenty-five animals, from ostrich to cow with a whole menagerie in between. Each animal, or bicho, was associated with four two-digit numbers that ran from 01 through 99, with the last number combination being 00. The players had to start by choosing an animal to bet on, how much they wanted to bet and how they wanted to do it. There were three daily drawings and five four-number combinations selected in each drawing. The players had to decide which of the five four-number combinations they wanted to bet on and for which of the three daily drawings, which were at one o'clock, four o'clock and seven o'clock each afternoon, rain or shine. If your animal's numbers were the last two digits of the particular combination that you had bet on, you won some multiple of your original bet.

You could also bet on all the digits of the four-number combo and the strategies sounded endless, from betting on an animal straight up to mixing and matching different combinations and even inverting combinations. I got dizzy listening to the explanation. As Anjo explained the rules to me in English, he asked for clarifications from Nelson and pretty soon a small group of interested parties was contributing ideas and sure winners. It was all delivered in pretty rapid-fire Portuguese, so I didn't get much out of it, but there was no shortage of confidence among the growing crowd. I pulled Anjo outside the circle for a second.

"Okay, Anj, I'll take some action, but just to soak up a little local atmosphere. How much do we bet and what animal do we take?"

"I always bet on the rooster and the lamb."

"Why's that?"

"They are the required sacrifices for Shango…"

"And you being a babalorixa of Shango, those would have to be your bets. Any luck with them?"

He shrugged his shoulders and gave me a wan smile. It was the universally understood gesture for "not really".

"That's comforting. What are my other choices?"

He started reciting the bichos and I stopped him when he said turkey.

"That's the one for me because that's exactly how I feel here in Salvador. How should we bet?"

"It is always best to do the most simple way the first time."

"You're right, let's keep it simple for the simpleminded. Okay, how about five reais on the turkey for each combination in the next drawing?"

"Are you sure you want to bet that much?"

"Sure, what the fuck? With all these experts helping us out, how can we lose? So that would be what, twenty-five reais? Just what I already lost today."

"Nelson will be very happy to make a sale. It's a long time that I don't play."

Anjo explained the bet to Nelson and this time his smile got wide enough to cover both Fifth and Madison Avenues when he saw me pull out the reais for the bet. He took it, went over to his outpost and came back with my receipt. I was amazed to see that it was a printed receipt that had the time of the drawing in the upper left-hand corner, the date in the upper right-hand corner, the group number that corresponded to my bicho in the center and the details of my bet. Nelson had kept his word about the discount by doubling the amount of my bet for free. The drawing was for four o'clock that afternoon.

"Anjo, when can we find out if we've won?"

"Anytime after four."

"You mean anytime after they've calculated which animal will mean the lowest payout and the highest profit to the guys that run this scam."

"Exactly."

"Just out of curiosity, what are the my winning number combinations?"

"The turkey is associated with the numbers seventy-seven, seventy-eight, seventy-nine and eighty."

"Those are some lucky-sounding numbers, my friend. Tell Nelson we'll be back later to collect my winnings."

Nelson gave me a big thumbs-up sign and I told him in Portuguese that it had been a pleasure. Anjo and I resumed our stroll down Chile Street. It was about three o'clock and I was getting hungry.

"Anj, can we get something to eat somewhere? I'm starving."

"I'm glad you asked. There is a very good restaurant on Rui Barbosa where we can get some feijoada and see the football game at the same time."

"It won't be too late to get a table?"

"Even if it is, I am friends with the owner and he will accommodate us."

"Shit, Anj, is there anybody in this town you're not friends with?"

CHAPTER 13

FIVE MINUTES LATER WE were seated in a hole in the wall that would have had to remodel itself to be called a dive. The entire restaurant was about the size of The White Horse Tavern's men's room. There were four tables and three were occupied by the employees staring at a black and white TV from the Cretaceous Epoch that was mounted on a triangular shelf in a corner about six feet off the ground. The picture was surprisingly sharp. I attributed the good reception to the quality of the clothes hangar sticking out of the top of the television. The tables were made of Formica with hollow metal legs. The plastic covering that clung stubbornly to a couple of seats looked like it might have matched the tabletops at one time. The walls were painted a mint green that would have been promoted as tropical in New York, but was most likely just the cheapest color at the paint store in Salvador. Nobody even looked at us as we sat down at the fourth table and Anjo immediately went into the same trance as the others. Five minutes later it was halftime. Everybody came over to hug Anjo, shake my hand, take our order and throw our food at us, all before the action started up again. I ordered two beers since the odds of getting service in the second half of a game tied at one goal each seemed stacked against my thirst. I could have taken all my clothes off and danced naked on the Formica and nobody would've noticed. About twenty minutes into the second half a collective groan from the crowd morphed into deep, lasting despair as the bad guys took a two to one lead. Mass suicide in the restaurant was narrowly avoided by a second goal from the hometown favorites. Then euphoria struck like a lightning bolt as the good guys took a three to two lead with only minutes left. I got a small taste of what Carnival must be like in Salvador when the game ended with that result. Everybody in the restaurant started jumping up and down with their arms in the air, screaming at the top of their lungs. Then they formed some kind of Brazilian conga line and danced their way out onto the sidewalk. They were joined by people spilling out of the other doorways on the street, all of them whooping like they had scored the winning goal themselves.

I stood in the doorway watching Anjo in his element. He was hugging all his fellow fans and clinking his beer bottle against any other bottle within reach. A boom box appeared playing some power samba music and small groups of people started dancing in the street. Rui Barbosa wasn't all that wide a street, but it wasn't a footpath, either. But it didn't matter because no vehicle was going to make it through this crowd without at minimum buying a round of beer for the celebrants.

In the midst of all the revelry, I thought I heard my name being called. Since Anjo had forgotten my existence for the moment, I looked to my left and saw Wanda Miranda, the woman whose pastries I had tried to purchase that morning. After two beers with feijoada, I felt my morning boldness returning, so I went all out with my Portuguese.

"Vahnda Meerahnda, comoo va-ee?"

She was so impressed with my Portuguese "Howyadoin" that she came back to me in English.

"I am good. And you?"

"Great. I'm just waiting for the party to end."

I gestured toward the dancers. She nodded.

"Why you no help Anjo with dance?"

I told her I'd had enough trouble for one day and pointed to the cut on my head. She was clearly impressed.

"Ay, what happen to you?"

I didn't think she wanted all the details, so I summed it up as best I could.

"Some kid hit me with a rock."

She narrowed her eyes at me and extended her hand.

"I touch."

It wasn't a question. I leaned over to let her reach my forehead. She had feathers for fingers, so there was no need for screeching on my part. She pulled her hand back after passing over the wound and thought for a second. She then reached into one of her bags and pulled out a small bag of herbs and two small ribbons, one red, one blue, tied together. She pressed the two things into my hand.

"When bed tonight, you put water on bag, then put on blood. Then you say 'Eu-eo' three times and put ribbon under pillow when go to sleep. Blood much better next day."

I was a little skeptical about folk cures, but she was a good friend of Anjo. What else could I say?

"Thank you, Wanda. I'll do that."

"You welcome. Now I must go. Boa tarde."

"Boa tar-gee."

She walked on down Rui Barbosa Street and turned left about fifty yards down. I noticed for the first time that her gait was somehow a little off. She wasn't limping, but it was like one of her legs was maybe slightly weaker than the other. Meanwhile, the sports celebration was finally winding down. I took the last sip of my beer as Anjo glided through the ever sparser crowd.

"So the good guys won, eh, Anjo?"

"It is the first time Esporte Clube Bahia has beaten Esporte Clube Vitoria in a long time and we are all supporters of Clube Bahia."

"That would explain the second coming of Carnival."

He grinned.

"It is not quite as good as the real Carnival, but it is very close."

He looked at my left hand and saw the bag of herbs and the two ribbons.

"Where did you get that?"

"From Wanda Miranda. She stopped by while you were celebrating."

"Did she tell you to put the herbs on the cut on your head?"

"She did."

"And to say 'Eu-eo' three times?"

"All that and the ribbons under my pillow when I go to sleep tonight."

He nodded.

"Good. That is very good."

"I have no doubts that it is, but would you mind letting me in on the secret here? How are the herbs and the ribbons going to cure a rock-induced head wound?"

"I do not know anything about the herbs she gave you. Wanda is a curandeira and knows how to cure many illnesses better than most doctors. She is a filha de santo of Ossaim, the orixa of medicines and cures. The red and blue ribbons she gave you are Ossaim's colors. The words she told you to say three times are the greeting for Ossaim. They will help ensure that Ossaim guides the positive effect of the herbs on your cut. You will wake up looking and feeling better tomorrow morning."

I had complete faith in what Anjo was telling me. I had witnessed first-hand the power of the orixas, the saints of the Brazilian religion of Candomble, during Anjo's visit to New York a couple of years before. One of the orixas had saved me from being turned into fish bait in the Hudson River. I was no expert on Brazilian culture, but I knew better than to doubt the orixas' capabilities, especially in Salvador, Brazil, their home turf. But I couldn't resist the opportunity to bust Anjo's chops a little.

"Yeah, well, if I wasn't continually getting assaulted whenever I work with you, I wouldn't need the herbs and special greetings to improve my looks and reduce my swelling."

He was too sharp to take my bait.

"Oy, Mike, I thought the favelas here in Brazil would be easy to handle for a New Yorker like you. You must be out of practice. Or maybe you are getting old."

"Anj, I'm thirty-four, so I left old behind a long time ago. I'm closing in on ancient. What else do you have in store for me today?"

"Since the football game is over, I think it would be a good time to visit the family of the third victim."

CHAPTER 14

HIS NAME WAS JORGE Arruda and his was the body that had been mutilated. As a light-skinned mulatto, he'd have been referred to as bi-racial in New York City, a politically correct term that would serve no purpose in Salvador since as near as I could tell, my cousin and I were the only people in the entire city that weren't a mixture of at least two races, and frankly, with Bones' permanent tan, I was beginning to have my doubts about him, too. Jorge had been a fare collector on the city buses that ran all over Salvador. I got the impression that it was a pretty good gig as jobs for the working poor went. He lived on Gregorio de Matos Street, which was back towards the Largo do Pelourinho from where we were. It was within walking distance, so we hoofed it from the restaurant.

The building was somewhat less than Park Avenue swanky, but light years away from what we'd already visited. First of all, it was a real building. It was narrow and looked to be about four stories tall. The façade was having a little difficulty holding off gravity, but the stairway leading up to the top floor was garbage and rodent free. The apartment had a real door and, from the sound of it, real locks on the inside. A kid of around eleven opened the door for us. He immediately embraced Anjo. He was about five feet tall with dark brown skin and tight curly hair. His name was Antonio. Anjo introduced me and the kid shook my hand with both of his while I mumbled a greeting in Portuguese, happy that he wasn't holding a rock. His mom's name was Sandra. She was a roundish woman of slightly darker complexion than her son who was also about five feet tall. She burst into tears when she saw Anjo and only stopped crying long enough to shake my hand. It took her another five minutes to calm down. When Anjo explained what we were there for, I hit her with all the same questions I had asked of Dona Eva and Maria. The answers I got back were about the same as well.

Jorge had gone out the Tuesday night he disappeared. He was hooking up with a couple of guys from work to have a beer or two and was supposed to be back home at eleven. He was another outgoing guy, a characteristic that seemed more and more like a requirement for living in Salvador. Another big surprise was that he occasionally lost track of time when having fun. His not showing up by midnight didn't set off any alarm bells with Sandra, so she had gone to bed at her normal time. He was still gone when she woke up the next day and that worried her because he was nothing if not punctual for work. She didn't say anything to Antonio, who left for school, but asked all the neighbors she could find if they knew anything. Nobody had seen Jorge come in at night or go out in the morning.

It was about ten o'clock when the buzz from the Igreja do Passo wafted over to her street. She had a bad feeling when she ran out of the building and it got worse with every step toward the church. She remembered seeing the cadaver, which the local cops hadn't bothered to cover with a sheet, and knowing instantly that it was Jorge by the clothes. The next thing she knew, somebody was reviving her back at her apartment. By that time somebody had pulled Antonio out of school and the poor kid was standing over her, worried about losing his mom the same day somebody had murdered his dad. It was a sad story, one I was getting tired of hearing. I asked about any possible problems Jorge might have had with people at work or in whatever social groups he ran with, but Sandra couldn't think of anything. The guy was more popular than Santa Claus. She gave me the names of the buddies Jorge had gone out with that Tuesday so I could track them down at their work. I asked her all the usual questions about illegal activities or friends involved in such, but according to Sandra, Jorge was clean. It was then time for what had been the most disappointing question on my list so far.

"Anjo, ask her what the police told her."

Anjo translated my question. After thinking for a very long ten seconds, she said that a cop at the church had told her not to get too close to the body. That was it. I found myself trying to rationalize the sloppy police work by thinking that at least someone with a badge spoke to her, but it didn't seem like much of an improvement. I looked at Anjo.

"My previous comment on your law enforcement system still stands."

He looked back at me, shaking his head.

"So does mine."

We talked for a couple more minutes with Sandra, but we had pretty much everything we could hope to get. I told her we would try to talk with Jorge's drinking buddies and anybody else at his workplace that might be able to help. Then we shook hands, Anjo hugged her and we made for the door. Antonio was waiting for us at the bottom of the stairs. He said something to Anjo and the two of them approached me. The kid looked up at me with haunted eyes and spoke in halting English.

"Thank you for coming. Please help us with my father dead."

It wasn't perfect English, but I got the message.

CHAPTER 15

IT WAS ABOUT FIVE o'clock when we started walking back toward Chile Street. I was beat. Overwhelming grief always has that effect on me and even with the side trip to soccer paradise, I had spent the majority of the day absorbing three different strains of it. I thought about dropping by the SS Bones down at the docks, but I needed to get off my feet. We arrived at Das Vassouras Street and in my fatigue-induced haze, I imagined somebody calling my name.

"Oy, Mike Breza."

Anjo heard it, too and we both looked around. It was his good buddy Nelson and he looked even happier to see us than he had before. He was practically shouting at Anjo and Anjo's eyes looked like spotlights. They didn't get any smaller when he turned to look at me.

"Mike, you won."

"What do you mean I won?"

"You won the jogo do bicho."

"What, the turkey number came up?"

"Five times! It came out in every combination."

It sounded good, but I needed some hard facts.

"So what did I win, a couple of reais?"

Anjo translated for Nelson, who burst into raucous laughter, which was then picked up and passed all around the corner by the regulars who couldn't believe the moron from New York didn't understand. Anjo had to catch his breath before relieving me of the burden of my ignorance.

"A couple of reais? No, my friend, much more than that. You bet five reais on each combination and your numbers came up in every one. That means you have won eighteen times five reais five times."

I was sure they could hear the rusty gears turning in my brain from ten blocks away, but I tried the calculation anyway and liked what I found.

"Holy shit! You mean four hundred fifty reais?"

"That is correct, my friend."

Nelson stepped forward and began slapping fives and tens into my sweaty palm. It was an impressive pile of bills. Suddenly my fatigue didn't seem so overwhelming. He gave me a big bear hug when he finished and said something to Anjo before heading back to his spot with a big smile on his face.

"What's he say, Anjo?"

Anjo's smile matched Nelson's tooth for tooth.

"He says he wants to play the same bichos as you next time."

My track record for epiphanies wasn't very good. The last one I'd had dated back to the third grade and consisted of the realization that ducking Sister Peter

Miriam at recess was going to be the key to avoiding expulsion from Our Lady of Lourdes Elementary School. Nonetheless, at that moment the scales fell from my eyes. I chased after Nelson and handed him fifty reais.

"Mooeetoo obreegadoo, Nelson."

His jaw dropped. I gave him another fifty reais and told him it was for drinks for all of his regulars. I pointed at them and made sure Anjo translated for me. Then I handed Anjo a hundred reais. I felt like a rock star and the standing ovation the corner crowd gave me didn't diminish the sensation. Anjo tried to give me his money back, but I refused.

"Anjo, it's yours. Share and share alike."

"This is very generous of you, Mike."

"Hey, I couldn't have done it without your help."

He thought for a second and smiled.

"You know, Mike, you are right. Perhaps you should give me another fifty."

As we turned away from the newspaper stand, I made a mental note to look up the Portuguese word for "chutzpah". I also noticed a dark car parked on the corner of Chile and Das Vassouras with two men in the front seat. There were about five or six cigarette butts on the ground by the passenger door, several of them still smoldering. After we passed on our way to the Hotel do Chile, I nudged Anjo.

"Anj, who would be watching Nelson's operation from that black car behind us?"

He shot a discreet look over his shoulder, then looked back at me.

"There are three kinds of people who observe a cambista like Nelson, those foolish enough to think about robbing him, those paid enough to protect him and those not paid enough to protect him. The men in that car belong to the third group."

"What does that make them?"

He smiled.

"The police."

We split up at the entrance to the Hotel do Chile after agreeing to meet down at Bones' boat at about seven-thirty. That would give me a chance to slobber on my pillow and try to find my second wind somewhere. On the way into the hotel, I saw João behind the front desk and asked him for my key. He handed it over with no extra charge for the chat.

"So how's your second day been?"

He asked the question looking at the cut on my head.

"A mixture of good and not so good, but it's a hell of a town."

"What's the not so good?"

"A bunch of sad stories and a rock to the head, that's all."

"Oh, so you went to talk to the families?"

I probably shouldn't have been surprised by the comment, but I had been flattering myself by thinking I was flying under everybody's radar.

"How'd you know that?"

"News relating to Anjo circulates fast around the center of town. Most people associated with his terreiro knew somebody was coming from New York to help him with some problems. It didn't take much effort to figure out which problems and it took even less to peg you as the helper."

He leaned over and addressed me in a fake whisper.

"White boys like you stand out around here."

"Especially those of us with a New York Yankees backpack."

He nodded and continued.

"I also heard you met Wanda Miranda. Twice."

"Yeah, she gave me some stuff to put on my forehead."

"Well, do what she says. I haven't seen her be wrong yet and I know her ten years."

I was beginning to feel like I should just ask him who had done the murders. He seemed to know everything else about my business. I decided to see how up to date he was. I took out my wad of reais and counted out some bills.

"You're pretty well informed, João, but did you know I won the jogo do bicho?"

He shook his head, impressed with my luck.

"I didn't know that, but I knew you'd played the turkey."

I handed him fifty reais. I was pleased to see that he was finally surprised by something I did.

"Hey, what's this for?"

"Think of it as a down payment for covering my back. I've got a feeling that as long as you're monitoring what I'm doing in Salvador, things aren't gonna get too bad for me down here."

Everybody should feel like a rock star once in a while.

CHAPTER 16

WHEN I WOKE UP from my nap at seven-fifteen, the rock star feeling had faded, but at least I felt human again. I wanted to attribute my fatigue to jet lag, but the one-hour time difference between Salvador and New York wasn't enough to pass for an excuse. A little cold water on my face got me ready to go.

I wasted less time getting down to the docks than the previous night and found Bones in more or less the same position on his boat. This time he saw me coming.

"Please spare me any embarrassing attempts at sounding nautical, okay?"

"My pleasure, Cap'n Crunch."

He tossed me a beer as I sat down next to him and eyed my forehead.

"How'd the rest of your day go?"

"More bad stories that involved little contact with the police, but too much contact with a rock. How'd your repairs go?

"It wasn't much really. Turned out I just needed a couple of fuses."

A familiar voice rang out from down below.

"Oy, senhores!"

Anjo came aboard with some beers under his arm. Bones was impressed.

"Hey, Anjo, you didn't have to do that. I've got plenty of beer as long as my cousin doesn't go back to his youthful habits of drinking non-stop."

"Oh, but I had to bring something to celebrate such a magnificent veleiro. Can I walk around to visit?"

"Sure, Anj, I'll show you around myself. Just let me give a couple of these Brahmas to the boys on the dock."

Bones walked over to the gangplank and shredded the night with another heart-stopping whistle. I still expected several cabs to show up, but all that appeared was one of the dock vigilantes who was very appreciative of what Bones handed over to him. Anjo and Bones then disappeared downstairs for the grand tour of the Sweet St. Pete and I was left alone with a beer and my thoughts on a tropical evening with the hint of a breeze sliding past me. It would've been the perfect end to the perfect day, if I'd had one. But I hadn't and what I did have didn't impress me so much. I was pretty sure Flavio Guimarães had been dragged off against his will since I had actually seen some evidence of this. I assumed the same thing had happened with both Carlos de Souza and Jorge Arruda, since nobody would be likely to volunteer for what had happened to them, but I had nothing but conjectures at this point. I did know that all three had turned up dead after torture on the steps of the Church of the Superholy Sacrament and that the loss to their families was strong and maybe insurmountable. What hadn't been strong was the effort of the cops to even start an investigation. Another breeze stroked my face. It was a gorgeous night in a beautiful tropical city as long as you didn't think about grisly unsolved murders.

Anjo and Bones came back up laughing their asses off. I asked what was so funny and sure enough, Bones was telling Anjo how I almost burned his house down by setting fire to his backyard when I was ten years old. The image of my old man hustling across the yard with a hose was almost as indelible as the welts on my ass that same hose raised shortly thereafter. It was Bones' imitation of me trying to sit down that tickled Anjo's funnybone.

"Okay, guys, vaudeville is dead and you two clowns sure aren't bringing it back. What about dinner?"

In between his last sputters of laughter, Anjo had an opinion.

"I know a place close to here that is not so expensive, eh?"

We followed Anjo off the boat and he led us to the Plaza Cayru, the same place we had eaten the previous night in the Modelo Market. He looked ready to cruise right through the plaza, but a new personal record for epiphanies on my part stopped him cold.

"Anjo, hold up a second. I need to step into Camafeu de Oxossi."

Bones couldn't believe my narrow-mindedness.

"Hey, Mike, we ate there yesterday."

"This isn't about the food, Cuz."

I left them in the center of the plaza, hustled over to the market and ran up the stairs. The hostess for the rival restaurant, Maria de São Pedro, was rounding up clients like they were giving away the grub, but I didn't see Wanda Miranda anywhere. Then I stepped inside the door to Camafeu and practically knocked her into the waiting bench on the side of the entrance.

"Wanda, I'm sorry. Me desculpe."

I couldn't tell if her smile was that of a professional hostess or if she actually recognized me, but it didn't take her long to erase my doubts.

"Boa noite, Mike Breza. You here to eat again?"

"No, I'm here to tell you that I won the jogo do bicho."

She smiled again.

"You played o peru. The turkey."

I couldn't believe my ears.

"Did they announce it on TV or something? How does everybody know about this?"

Her smile turned into a laugh.

"No TV, but I speak with João in the Hotel do Chile and he say to me."

I reached into my pocket and took out one hundred reais.

"Look, Wanda, this is for you. For the pastries, for the cure you gave me and even more for letting me practice my Portuguese with you without laughing in my face."

She started to shake her head, but I grabbed her hand and forced the bills into it.

"Look, either you take the money or I leave it here on the floor. Okay?"

This time she relented.

"Thank you, Mike Breza. Muito obrigada."

"You're welcome, Wanda."

I pulled open the door and went back across the plaza to hook back up with Anjo and Bones. Anjo was nodding his head when I got there.

"Mike, you just gave Wanda some of your money from the jogo do bicho, right?"

"You got it, boss."

"You are a very good man, Mike Breza."

I wasn't convinced, but had to admit that I didn't feel half bad.

CHAPER 17

THE RESTAURANT ANJO TOOK us to was another marvel of backstreet Salvador. If you didn't know where to look, you couldn't find this place even with a Geiger counter. It was in the vicinity of the Lacerda Elevator, but it looked more like somebody's house than a restaurant. Maybe that's why the food was so damn good and so damn cheap. We ate fish, sausage and beef along with beer and some green things that were promoted as vegetables, but that had definitely never been sold legally in any store in New York City. Not even Chinatown. I even ordered a cafezinho, feeling foolishly confident that my fatigue wasn't going to be challenged by anything as pedestrian as caffeine. After an hour of boat talk, I felt it was time to set up the next day's schedule.

"Anjo, what do you have planned for tomorrow?"

He shrugged and sipped his cafezinho.

"I will plan whatever you feel should be the next step."

"Well, I was thinking that tomorrow would be a good day to talk with the police to see if they can tell us anything about the investigations."

His eyes widened the slightest bit and I could tell he didn't like the idea.

"Mike, the police will not help us on these cases. They will not tell us anything."

"I agree with you, but my experience is that sometimes you learn more from people who don't want to help you and sometimes it's what people don't say that turns out to be the most valuable information. Do you know anyone who can ignore us down at police headquarters?"

He rubbed his face and put his toothpick to work with the dexterity of an oral surgeon.

"Mike, the only police official who has even mentioned the case was the head of the police for the city. He only did it because there were complaints from the owners of stores near where the bodies were left. In all of the newspaper articles about the crimes, I cannot even think of a single police official who has been named as the head of the investigation. I think the best thing to do is go to the police station and ask for someone to help us."

If the Salvador police bureaucracy operated with the same kind of efficiency as the homicide detectives supposedly investigating the case, we were going to be in for a long day. But what the hell else did I have to do with my time?

"Okay, Anj, what time can we go visit police headquarters?"

"Perhaps nine-thirty."

"It's a date. Gents, the meal is on our good friend, Nelson, he of the jogo do bicho."

It cost me all of fifty reais, which meant that I was back to even on the day. My bad luck with little kids had been offset by good karma with little pictures of animals. We walked out of the restaurant into a beautiful Salvador night. The streets were populated, but not percolating like the night before. Even in Brazil, the weekend started to wind down on Sunday night.

"So, guys, nine o'clock at the hotel for breakfast, then on to police headquarters for a little game of twenty questions?"

Bones and Anjo were amenable and we split up for the night. I walked back to the Lacerda Elevator and rode up to Chile Street. I turned right out of the elevator and in half a block was at the corner of Vassouras and Chile. I didn't see my benefactor Nelson, but there was a group of guys hanging around the same general vicinity. There was also the same dark car parked in the same spot with what looked like the same population inside. I thanked my lucky stars it wasn't me doing the boring-ass surveillance work and finished my evening stroll by stepping into my deluxe Hotel do Chile accommodations. I peeled off my clothes and found the bag Wanda Miranda had given me, along with the red and blue ribbons. I figured what the heck and wet the bag before setting it gingerly on the deluxe wound on my forehead. I laid back and dozed off for a few minutes before waking up with a start. The herbs fell in my lap and I gave up. I looked around the room to make sure there was no camera recording my foolishness for blackmail purposes, said "eu-eo" three times and put the ribbons under my pillow. Then I fell out of the world.

There was plenty of sun streaming in my window at eight o'clock the next morning. I knew I was getting used to local time because it didn't seem so hostile to me. I looked around the room and felt like I knew where I was, another sign of progress. But the real surprise came when I actually looked at myself in the mirror. The face staring back at me had practically no head wound to speak of. There was a mark and maybe a slight swelling, but no sign of blood, dried or otherwise, and no visible sign of the skin being broken. My first thought was that the herbs in the bag were worth their weight in gold. My second thought was that if I could get those herbs back to New York City, I'd make a killing selling them in bodegas citywide. I shaved, showered and got dressed with the energy only a future import/export millionaire could have.

It was about twenty minutes before nine when I got down to the lobby. There was nobody to greet me, but I was far from disappointed. I had it in mind to take a quick walk to see what I could see, then kill my hunger with breakfast. João wasn't at the front desk when I walked by, so I breezed out the door to the right and almost leveled a woman walking down the sidewalk. That was my first surprise. My second was when she spoke.

"Seu Mike Breza."

She was gorgeous and any town where gorgeous women that you practically run over know your name and smile at you is a place that I want to live. I made a mental note to have my brother ship all four of my possessions to Brazil, then took a closer look at my almost victim. It took me a couple of seconds to place her, but I managed to figure it out.

"Teresa?"

"Sou. Como vai?"

I wanted to tell her that I'd very rarely been better than I was at that moment looking at her dressed in white pants and a red shirt that were no doubt in clothing heaven clinging as they were to her legs, hips and torso. I wanted to tell her that, but my Portuguese in a state of surprise was even weaker than it normally was and all I managed to produce was a guttural sound that had no relation with human speech. She made me feel worse by continuing to smile at me, or maybe she was used to that kind of reaction from men. At any rate, I finally got around to stammering that I was fine and asking her how she was. My mom would have been proud of me for my politeness, delayed though it may have been. I understood her to say that she was fine and that it was a beautiful morning. I already knew that, but it had nothing to do with the weather. My brain freeze then lifted, so I asked her what she was doing there. Of course, I had to ask her twice to get her to understand me, but I gathered that she worked nearby as a maid in someone's house. She acted like she had something else to say, but since I couldn't imagine what it might be, I took the heat off her and asked if she wanted to have a morning cafezinho with me. She nodded her head, leaving me with the problem of figuring out how I could make good on the offer since I could only remember how to get to the restaurants down by the dock. That's when she took the heat off me, partially at least, by saying we might be able to get some coffee in the hotel six feet behind me.

When we stepped back inside the Hotel do Chile, João was behind the front desk. He nodded his head in approval at the sight of Teresa.

"Bom dia, Mike. Bom dia, senhora."

We both responded in kind and I continued in English.

"João, is it too early to get some cafezinhos for my friend, Teresa, and me?"

He consulted his fake Rolex, undoubtedly purchased during his time in New York City.

"Looks like the perfect moment to me. Follow me into the dining room. This way. Por aqui, senhora."

It was my first look at the Hotel do Chile's dining area and it wasn't half bad. There were about seven tables, two of which were for couples, while the others all seated four. On the left was a big window with a whole lot of sun roaring in and in front of the entrance was the kitchen where João disappeared while I held Teresa's chair for her, just like my mom had smacked into my head over twenty-one years of living at home. I felt pretty confident until I found myself face to face with her.

Maybe it had been the light in Dona Maria's shanty or maybe I had been too focused on business at the time, but in the morning sun I saw that Teresa had the most beautiful skin I'd ever seen. It was like flawless black porcelain and the Greeks had laid siege to Troy for less than the beauty of her facial features. If João hadn't shown up in that instant with two cafezinhos, I probably wouldn't have been able to make a sound.

"Dois cafezinhos. I have to go back to the front desk."

"Thanks, João."

She lifted the cafezinho to her mouth and the idea of being a small white cup in that moment held a certain appeal for me. Before I could take a hit of my own cafezinho, Teresa started to talk. Fortunately, she talked slowly.

It turned out that she wanted to apologize again for her son and his posse mugging me the previous day. I aw-shucksed it a little bit, telling her not to worry about it, that I should have know better than to wander around a favela without a local guide. It was at that point that she looked at my forehead, amazed that there was practically no mark at all. I explained as best as I could that a curandeira had given me some herbs from Ossaim that had really cleaned me up. She nodded her head while I struggled through the Portuguese, then spoke two words when I finished.

"Wanda Miranda."

She was right and I told her so. She told me that Wanda was the best curandeira around. Lots of people from all socioeconomic levels preferred her work over even the best doctors in the city. She was always willing to help, but the trick was finding her. She didn't seem to have any fixed address, although the feeling was that she lived somewhere in the Pelourinho district. The one thing everybody knew was that she sold her pastries daily on Ajuda Street, where I'd seen her the previous morning. Her medical clientele normally tracked her down there as well, but after peddling hours she was a ghost, drifting around the city haphazardly, turning up unexpectedly. I was going to mention how she had appeared at the soccer celebration the day before, but Teresa glanced at her watch and jumped to her feet.

"Me desculpe, Mike. Tenho de ir agora mesmo para não chegar tarde ao trabalho."

I didn't want her to be late for work, so I walked her quickly back to the hotel entrance. When we got there I thanked her for coming by and offered her my hand, which she ignored. She gave me a kiss on both cheeks and I got the impression that if I had turned my head slightly to one side or the other she wouldn't have hesitated to put the kisses on my lips. She practically ran out the door afterward. I stepped out to watch her as she walked away, thinking that maybe she'd look back. She didn't disappoint me. She looked back and saw me watching her. I hoped I hadn't disappointed her either.

CHAPER 18

I TURNED AROUND TO step back inside the hotel and this time I almost flattened Anjo, who had apparently come up from the other direction just in time to see me watching Teresa.

"She is attractive, no?"

"She is attractive, yes. She came by to apologize again for her kid assaulting me."

Anjo smiled.

"I do not think that is the only reason she came."

My imagination was running on all cylinders, so I didn't need to ask him what other reason she might've had for coming by. I marked it down as just another reason to move to Salvador when my work was done. I suggested to Anjo that we grab some breakfast in the friendly confines of the Hotel do Chile. It sounded good to him and we stepped inside. As we passed the front desk, João started shaking his head with a pained expression on his face.

"Oy, Mike, you have made a bad trade. Your first guest was prettier."

I didn't argue the point.

We sat at one of the four person tables in the dining room just out of the reach of the sun, which was promising another beautiful day in Salvador. We had just grabbed the one sheet menu when João escorted Bones into the room. As he left, João looked back for one last comment.

"Mike, you start your breakfast with a beautiful woman. Then you change to Anjo. Then you add your cousin. You are going from bad to worse, my friend."

Bones wasn't sure what to make of the comment, but the menu was calling so I didn't have to explain. It was cafezinhos and eggs all around and the recently-arrived waiter hustled off to the kitchen for us. It was a good time for me to get my bearings on the day's work.

"So, Anjo, where are we going and who can we speak with?"

"I believe the delegacia we need to visit is the one on Rua Alfredo de Brito since it is the closest to the Pelourinho."

He'd lost me at the fourth word of his sentence.

"Anj, what's a deh-leh-gah-see-ah?"

Bones nudged me and used his best fake stage whisper.

"It's the police station. Just pretend you understand."

"Got it. Just trying to keep up with you linguistic Einsteins, that's all. Do we know who we have to talk to?"

Anjo shook his head as the eggs appeared in front of us along with three glasses of water and a second round of cafezinhos.

"I have not been able to find out the name of the delegado, excuse me, the detective in charge of the cases."

"So what do we do, just ask for the homicide department?"

"I think that would be the best idea."

Anjo explained that under the police system in Brazil, the delegado is the official in charge of a group of detectives who investigate a crime. The delegado oversees the case until its end and is the person ultimately responsible for the final result.

"So we need to go to the police station and ask who the clown is that hasn't lifted a finger in trying to solve these murders, right?"

Anjo nodded, but offered me some sage advice at the same time.

"Perhaps we should not use the word clown in asking for the delegado."

Bones smiled at me.

"He knows you well, Cuz. I might refrain from saying 'fuck' too much as well."

It wasn't easy living down a hard-earned reputation like mine.

Alfredo de Brito Street was on the way to the Pelourinho District and the path took us past Das Vassouras Street, the site of my big gambling winnings of the previous day. As we walked by, to a man, the entire corner crowd shouted and beckoned for us to come over. I looked at Anjo and he gave me a why-not shrug. The black car from the day before was nowhere in sight, so we took a slight detour from the trip to the police station.

Nelson rose from his seat and was the first to squeeze the breath out of me with an affection borne of fifty reais in his own pocket. I was then subjected to the same treatment by a Jose, a Jesse, a Wilson and a host of other drinkers that had benefited from my largesse the previous evening. To alleviate the wear and tear on my ribcage, I introduced Bones as my cousin and watched him get the same treatment. I was back to rock star status, but I had a feeling it wasn't going to last. Nelson asked me how what animal I wanted to play. I looked at Anjo.

"Hey, Anj, do I have to play?"

He shook his head.

"You do not have to, but after winning, you should play until you lose, then stop if you wish."

I looked at my cousin.

"Bones, what do you think?"

He shrugged.

"Mike, you're still in Salvador."

It was the perfect attitude to rationalize risking another twenty-five reais.

"Okay, Anjo, I'm in."

I explained to Nelson as best as I could that I wanted to place the same bet as the day before, five reais on the turkey for each combination in the one o'clock drawing. The moan of disappointment that went up from the corner crowd told me they were pretty unhappy with my choice. Wilson even grabbed Anjo's ear and pleaded with him to make me change my mind. After what sounded like a blistering critique of my strategy, Anjo turned around.

"Wilson says it's a foolish bet."

"Why's that?"

"The same animal is almost never drawn on consecutive days. He thinks you should pick something different."

"With all due respect to Wilson, I don't believe that his lifetime winning percentage in this game is anywhere near mine. I believe my strategy is sound and I'm gonna stick with it."

I turned to look Nelson in the eye.

"And besides, Nelson is going to double my bet for me, just like yesterday. Right, Nelson?"

Anjo explained what I'd said and even if Nelson hadn't wanted to do it, the hooting from the corner crowd would've forced his hand. Nelson looked at me with eyes that said "another crazy gingo", took my money, gave me a receipt and wished me good luck. He sounded like he thought I was really going to need it this time. I looked at Anjo.

"Okay, Anj, how long until the one o'clock drawing?"

"Two hours from now."

"Okay, so we have plenty of time to go over to police headquarters and chat before everyone has a big laugh because I chose the same animal, right?"

"That is correct."

"All right, so let's get going. I wouldn't want these guys to miss their daily chuckles."

CHAPTER 19

WE WERE CROSSING THE Praça da Se on our way to Alfredo de Brito Street when I remembered that I had no real plan for talking to whomever was in charge of the homicides, if anybody.

"Anjo, how are we going to convince this detective to talk to us?"

"Well, he is not a detective, he is a delegado, more like a supervisor of detectives."

"Will that make him more willing to talk to us?"

He shook his head.

"No, it will probably make him less willing."

I could see that there wasn't any easy solution in the offering. We were in front of police headquarters with no original ideas, so I decided to rely on an old chestnut. I motioned for Bones and Anjo to come closer.

"Okay, guys, here's the play. Bones, you and I are freelance journalists from New York on vacation in Brazil. Anjo was our taxi driver, we got wind of the murders and decided it would make a great article for one of our hometown newspapers or magazines. Anjo, you'll be doing most of the talking, so just translate what I say. Bones, you just nod your head and look journalistic. Got it?"

They looked at me like they thought I knew what I was doing. I felt good that I was at least fooling someone. I took my notebook out of my backpack to look more professional and we marched inside.

The entrance was so dimly lit that we could've been in the Sixth Precinct on Tenth Street in Manhattan. Bones and I sat on the prehistoric waiting chairs while Anjo walked over to the reception desk. The desk jockey parked there rolled his eyes like every cop who ever sat behind the entrance desk in every police station in the world as Anjo told our story. When Anjo didn't move, the guy tried looking every which way except right at him in the hopes that this would make Anjo disappear. When that didn't work, he tried pretending he was looking for something on his desk. At this point, Anjo leaned in a little closer and whispered something that made the cop jerk to attention and listen. Anjo said something else, the cop stepped down nodding his head and faded into the back room calling someone's name. Anjo came back over to us with the broadest of smiles.

"Anj, what'd you say that made him jump like that?"

"I told him I was from the Terreiro do Morro and reminded him that Shango is a very impatient orixa."

Bones looked over at me with a grin.

"It's all about the connections, Cuz."

Five minutes later the same desk jockey rode back into view, motioning for us to follow him. He led us down a hall to a windowless room whose décor was early interrogation and left us there. I wasn't sure if I should sit down or smoke a last cigarette. Then the door swung open followed by two men in suits. The older guy was about my height with coal black hair parted on the side. He had an even blacker don't-fuck-with-me moustache that stopped abruptly at the borders of his lips. He looked to be in his forties, with just a hint of crow's feet forming at the edges of a pair of brown eyes. His skin was about the same color as Bones', but without the solar exposure. He had some kind of pad and a pencil in his hand. His sidekick was younger and probably shaved only about once every lunar month. If he'd shown up in my bar, I would've carded him every time and even then I might not have served him. His brown eyes looked out from deep sockets set in copper-colored skin. His hair was cropped close to the bone, but would've probably exploded into Manny Ramirez curls if he let it. Neither of them looked particularly friendly, but I didn't pick up on any hostility either. They were probably just being cops. The older detective spoke first. All I understood was that his name was Neto. He immediately understood that Bones and I spoke limited Portuguese and switched to an impressive English.

"Forgive me. I did not realize that you do not speak Portuguese. I am Delegado Antonio Neto and this is Detective Carlos Santos."

The younger detective gave us a barely perceptible nod. Detective Neto continued.

"I understand that you are journalists. How can we help you?"

That was my cue.

"First of all, Delegado Neto, thank you for taking time to meet with us. My name is Mike Breza and my partner, Gary Renfrow, and I are free-lance journalists in New York. We're down here on vacation and Anjo Denovo here told us about some unsolved murders in Salvador that we thought might make a good story to sell back in New York. Would it be all right if we asked you some questions about them?"

When I mentioned Anjo's name, both detectives shifted their eyes momentarily in his direction. It looked like a throwaway glance, but they definitely filed his face away for future reference. Neto responded with a question while he doodled on his pad.

"Do you have some journalistic credentials?"

It was the right first question, but I had my answer.

"Actually, as free-lance journalists, we're not technically employees of any particular newspaper. We write articles that we think could be of interest to New York newspapers and try to sell them to the highest bidder."

"I see. And what unsolved murders are you interested in asking about?"

I flipped open my notebook.

"Those would be the murders of Flavio Guimarães, Carlos de Souza and Jorge Arruda."

His eyes narrowed at the sound of the three names.

"I believe those are murders that are still being investigated."

"Well, that's why I used the word 'unsolved'. We were just wondering…"

He cut me off, but fast.

"I'm sorry, Mr., uh, uh"

"Breza, Mike Breza."

"I'm sorry, Mr. Breza, but I cannot comment on investigations that are still underway."

He was getting ready to run us out of his office. I could feel it.

"Well, then can you comment on the coincidence that all three bodies had whip marks on them and that each victim had a swastika carved into his back? Can you comment on all three bodies being dumped on the steps in front of the Rua do Passo Church in the Pelourinho district?"

He shook his head, smiling.

"Well, then, can you comment on that fact that no police official ever talked to any of the spouses of the murdered men? Is there a reason that Salvador detectives don't care enough to even pretend to gather information on the deceased?"

Bones was looking at me with the widest eyes I'd ever seen. Anjo was doing everything he possibly could to not look at me. Neto was still smiling as he pushed his chair away from the table in preparation for standing up.

"It is time for you to leave."

"Can you comment on the fact that all three victims were poor and black? Can you comment on any of these coincidences? Or is it beyond the capabilities of the Salvador Police Department to notice such similarities?"

Neto was still smiling as he opened the door for us. I was actually kind of relieved since I was running out of nasty questions. Bones and Anjo hurried out, but I dragged my feet a little to get a look at Detective Santos, who was studying the tops of his shoes. Unlike his supervisor, he was getting a little flushed, like the tone of my questions was getting under his skin a little. I figured I had nothing to lose.

"Detective Santos, can you respond to any of these questions?"

He looked up with a start. I stopped walking toward the door.

"Detective Santos, you know something about this case, don't you? Can you tell me why no progress has been made? Can you tell me why nobody here seems to give a shit about the deaths of three human beings?"

Neto's hand came down firmly on my shoulder to spin me around, but not before I made note of Detective Santos' young deer in the headlights imitation. Delegado Neto pushed me out the door in front of him.

"Mr. Breza, I would advise you to leave the police station immediately and I think you would be better off not pursuing your story."

I had nothing more to gain from infuriating him further, so I dropped the antagonistic act.

"If you insist, Delegado Neto."

He lowered the room's temperature with one more smile.

"I do insist, Mr. Breza."

With that, he was gone and I was in the waiting room with Bones, Anjo and the Willie Shoemaker of desk jockeys. They had somehow lost their timidity and were now looking at me once again as we stepped out into the street. Incredulity wasn't a strong enough word to describe their frame of mind. Bones was the first to recover his voice.

"Mike, what the fuck was that?"

I knew exactly what he meant, but my antagonistic mood hadn't totally dissipated.

"What do you mean?"

Eye-rolling was a Bones specialty and he didn't let me down.

"Give me a fucking break, man. You know damn well what I'm talking about. You just got finished giving major lip to a police officer in Brazil! And he wasn't some beat cop, he was a fucking chief of detectives! You're not in New York, Mikey! Cops do things here practically consequence-free. People disappear in this country all the time without a trace and nobody bats an eye. It took a major massacre of street kids in Rio to even make the papers and that was years after the fact! One missing American wouldn't budge anybody's give-a-shit meter in this country. Ask Anjo if you don't believe me."

Anjo was nodding in cadence with Bones' words.

"Your cousin is right, Mike. The police are very powerful here in Brazil. It was not a good idea to speak with such force to Delegado Neto. He can make very big problems for you."

Neither of them was telling me anything I couldn't have guessed on my own. Then Anjo, as always, surprised me.

"However, in spite of the problems he can make, I must tell you that I enjoyed very much listening to you give him your lip. It is not something that happens every day here in Salvador."

His grin of delight told me he wasn't just kidding.

"Well, I'm glad you enjoyed the show. My initial intention was just to poke him a little bit to see if I could learn something useful, but when it started looking like a dead end…"

Bones knew how the story had always ended.

"You figured what the fuck and just blasted the guy with no concern at all for whether it was the right thing to do or not."

"Well, yeah, pretty much."

Bones shook his head, but this time he was grinning.

"Same old Breza shit. Just like always."

"Consistency counts, Cuz."

"Yeah, okay, but I'm gonna get my boat sea-ready as fast as possible in case I have to slip out of town in the dead of night."

I looked over at Anjo.

"How about you, Anj? You gonna leave town, too?"

He shook his head.

"If I leave Salvador, there will be no one here to visit you na cadeia, I mean in prison, if you keep talking that way to delegados. And who would place flowers on your grave?"

He patted me on the shoulder.

"No, my New York friend, I will stay here in Salvador, no matter how badly you treat the police."

He looked over at Bones and they nodded to each other. The message had been delivered. The question was if I would remember to mind my manners in the future.

"Okay, guys, I got it. I'll try to rein myself in."

Bones wasn't sure that was an adequate promise.

"Actually, Mike, it might be a little more helpful if you would just stop being an asshole to the police, both collectively and individually."

CHAPTER 20

SEEING AS HOW OUR meeting with the delegado had been such an unqualified success, there was no longer any reason to stick around police headquarters. For lack of a better destination, we started walking vaguely back toward the Hotel do Chile. From at least a block away from Das Vassouras Street we could see that something was going on. There were all kinds of people gathered on the corner with more coming from every direction. The buzz of the growing crowd got louder the closer we got. Bones and I needed a cultural clue.

"Anjo, any idea of what might be going on?"

He was looking intently at the throng as we closed in, trying to come up with an explanation.

"I have only seen groups of people like this for celebrations of some kind. Maybe for football or…"

He snapped his wrist like a whip, his index finger smacking against the middle finger with a pop that sounded like somebody's face being slapped.

"That is Nelson's corner. Somebody must have won the jogo do bicho."

He looked at his watch. People were still arriving for the celebration.

"It is one-thirty. The results of the drawing must be out. Somebody won very big. That's why so many people are here."

"Well, let's go check it out."

We hustled on over. There must have been fifty people gathered around Nelson's newspaper stand. We stayed on the outside trying to see who the big winner at the center was, but we could only see Nelson and a couple of his cohorts jumping up and down. Then Nelson saw us.

"MIKE BREZA!!!"

I'd been in the country long enough to recognize my own name, especially when shouted, but I still hadn't absorbed the lesson on what to do when it happened. Fortunately Nelson took care of that for me. He rushed over to me as best he could through the mass of well-wishers and grabbed me in a bear hug that was extreme even by Brazilian standards. I was just about to lose consciousness when his shouts finally sank in. He was yelling over and over that I had won. When he finally let me go and I could enjoy the simple pleasure of oxygen once more, Bones grabbed my shoulder and pierced my eardrum with his own screeching.

"Mike you won the jogo do bicho!"

Anjo practically jumped into my arms.

"Voce ganhou, Mike. You won the jogo do bicho! Porra!"

"I won again? But how? You yourself told me nobody wins twice in a row with the same bet!"

I was sure it was going to be the only time in my life that my smile would out-shine Anjo's. He gave me the happiest shrug of his life.

"Oy and what the hell do I know about the jogo do bicho? You've already won as much in two days as I've won in twenty years of bad choices."

Hands were clapping on my shoulders like rain falling from the sky. I recognized most of Nelson's usual corner boys; Jesse, Jose and my pal Wilson, who had personally told me what a foolish bet I had placed. I caught his eye and he gave me a hearty Brazilian thumbs up, like he knew all along it was going to turn out this way. I grabbed Anjo's arm and pulled him over.

"Anjo, how much did we win?"

"Not we, my friend, you! The same as before, 450 reais."

"Can we get maybe a hundred of it and buy some drinks for this crowd?"

"Now you are thinking like a Brazilian!"

He went over and whispered the idea to Nelson, who was happy to oblige by taking a couple of cases of beer out of the refrigerator in the back of his newspaper stand. He passed them out, telling everybody that it was compliments of the big winner, Mike Breza. This led to another round of shoulder slaps and hugs from my new group of best friends for life. Somebody pulled out a boom box and some power samba music by some guy named Carlinhos Brown stoked the party up to full flame, with people dancing on the sidewalk and spilling into the mercifully slow traffic. I had Nelson distribute another case of beer and the party continued for another forty minutes before people started to drift away, disillusioned with the fact that it was still only Monday afternoon. I was leaning against a tree with a beer in my hand when I felt yet another hand on my shoulder from behind. This time the touch was lighter. It was Wanda Miranda.

"You have very good luck, Mike Breza."

"You know, Wanda, I'm almost ready to believe that."

"You are very generoso with your money."

"I wish I had more."

She smiled at me.

"I know you gave some money to Anjo and also to João. Nelson, too."

"Hey, Wanda, they all deserved it. And you did, too, for curing that lump on my forehead."

"But that is what I do."

"Well, sometimes I do the right thing, too. Not often, but enough to get by."

"You are a good man, Mike Breza."

"Do me a favor and keep telling people that, Wanda. I need all the friends I can get."

At that moment Anjo came over and threw a big hug around Wanda. They spoke a speed-of-light Portuguese of which I understood nothing and the conversation ended with Wanda saying "chow" or something like that. She also looked over at me and waved.

"Tchau, Mike Breza."

"Take care, Wanda."

Bones came over and gave me my umpteenth slap on the shoulder. It was one of those slaps that was just a little too hard to come from a completely sober man.

"Great street party, Cuz. Nice touch with the beer."

"I was due to make some friends after our warm and fuzzy sit-down with Delegado Neto."

"Well, if it's any consolation to you, I'm sure all these folks will be on your side right up until the money runs out."

"Just like New York."

"And everywhere else."

Anjo joined in.

"Oy, Mike, Bones, this was a good way to forget the problems with Delegado Neto, no?"

Bones cracked a wide smile.

"We were just saying the same thing."

"Anjo, any idea of how much money I've got left?"

He called Nelson, who gladly forked over three hundred fifty reais. I gave him fifty and kept fifty for myself. Then I gave the rest to Anjo, who started to protest.

"No, Mike, I cannot take your money again."

"That's good because it's not for you. I want you to take it and divide it up among the three widows you've introduced me to. They can make better use of it than I can."

Anjo and Bones stared at me for the second time that day with incredulity in their eyes. Anjo started to stammer a little.

"M-M-Mike…"

"Anjo, just divvy it up evenly between the three women. That's a little over eighty reais a head if I've figured it right. Give it to them the next time you see them, okay?

He was still staring at me, but at least he'd stopped stammering.

"I will do that, Mike. This is very kind of you."

"Yeah, well every other decade I try to do the right thing. How about we get some lunch with the remaining cash?"

Bones was ready.

"Good idea. I'm starving after having those beers. Anj, can we go back to where we saw the game yesterday?"

Anjo nodded, so we turned around to start toward Rui Barbosa Street. As we did so, I saw my favorite dark sedan parked in the same spot on Chile Street. This time, however, the two guys were actually four and they were standing around the car smoking cigarettes. They were also making a point of looking right at us as we walked by and not in a neighborly way. I nodded at them, but got no reaction, unless exhaling cheap cigarette smoke out the side of their mouths counted. When we reached the restaurant, I touched on the subject.

"Anjo, I still don't really understand what those cops are doing hanging around Nelson's corner. Are they protection or trouble or what? "

Anjo sipped his beer and answered me.

"Before I say anything, I wish to make clear that I do not fully understand how the jogo works."

Bones and I looked at each other.

"Sounds fair. So how do you think it works?"

"As I told you once before, the jogo do bicho is not legal, but it is tolerated. Here in Brazil, that tolerance sometimes has a price."

"You mean the cambistas pay off the cops?"

I was very proud of myself for using some of the local vocabulary.

"Sometimes there are bribes paid to the police, but they usually go to the more important officers and the money for those bribes doesn't come from the cambistas. It comes from those who truly control the game."

"Okay, so it comes in at an executive level and then gets distributed below."

Anjo smiled, but it wasn't really a hundred watts worth.

"That is the theory. Many times it doesn't work out that way and the street police receive nothing. They then have some choices."

"Which are?"

"They can either look for an opportunity to intimidate a cambista into paying them money to leave him alone or they can offer to protect him for a price."

"Is there a difference?"

"Sometimes. Sometimes the police really do protect the cambista by watching his corner as the police in the black car were doing. But sometimes the police watch to wait for a chance to attack the cambista."

"So what were our friends doing?"

"From the way they were looking at us as we passed, I do not think they were protecting Nelson."

"Yeah, well, from the way they were looking at us, I'd guess they're not very interested in protecting us either. As a matter of fact, I'd guess that they're more interested in thumping our heads. What do you think, Bones?"

"I think it's another one of your signature Mike Breza performances, leaving no stone unturned in your efforts to piss off every level of the Brazilian police hierarchy."

The only thing worse than a know-it-all cousin is one who happens to be right. Fortunately, the sandwiches arrived so I could conveniently stuff one in my mouth instead of answering.

The food was as good as it had been every place we'd eaten in Salvador and it was three o'clock by the time we finished. Anjo had to do some taxi driving to pay the rent and Bones had to supervise some maintenance on his boat. That left me by my lonesome to wander back to the Hotel do Chile and sleep off too many mid-afternoon beers and try to think about what my next move would be.

CHAPTER 21

João wasn't in the lobby to tell me how to run my life for the next few hours, so I had to go up to my room and figure it out for myself. I opened the shutters to my window, then flopped on my bed to think. The thinking part didn't take long since the cops weren't likely to help me at that point and the only fraction of a clue I had was a series of swastikas carved into three human backs. I felt my eyes closing and let it happen since the swastika was one of my least favorite symbols of all time. I was just starting to drift away when it hit me. If I were pursuing a case involving a swastika in New York, the first thing I'd do would be to consult with some authority on hate groups like the Southern Poverty Law Center or somebody else with a database on whatever racist groups might be operating in the New York area. It seemed a little incongruous to me that similar groups could exist in Brazil, a country where even the president claimed to have African ancestors, but I'd learned a long time ago not to underestimate human irrationality when it came to race. I needed to check the mother of all worldly information, the Internet.

I stood up from my bed and practically fell over. You'd think that a man who made his living serving alcohol to others would have the sense to rise a little more slowly from a prone position after several beers in the afternoon sun. Some cold water on my face helped me recover enough of my equilibrium to go downstairs. This time I found João manning the front desk.

"Hey, João, boa tarde."

"Oy, seu Mike Breza, como vai?"

"I'm good, man, but I need some help."

"I'm your man, Mike."

"Well, for starters, can I get a cafezinho and a cold glass of water?"

"A little caffeine to balance out the beer? Sounds like a good idea to me. Congratulations on winning the jogo do bicho again. I've never heard of anybody winning the same bet two days in a row. The orixas must be watching over you."

"They're more likely watching over Anjo and I'm just getting some of his overflow."

He yelled something into the office behind the counter and stepped out with me.

"Come on, Mike, let's get you a cafezinho."

We walked back to the restaurant, which was deserted at four-thirty in the afternoon, and he pointed me to a seat by the window.

"I'll be right back."

He wasn't kidding and two minutes later I had my little cup of jet fuel along with a two pint glass of water.

João served himself a cafezinho as well. I drained half the water glass while he was still adding sugar to his mud.

"So, Mike, how can I help you?"

"João, is there some kind of Internet café nearby? I need to get online and get some information."

He looked disappointed.

"That's it? That's all the help you want from me? How am I going to earn that money you gave me yesterday if this is all you want from me?"

I was going to say something, but he wasn't done.

"There is an Internet café four doors down to the left on Rua Chile. You can get another cafezinho and use their laptops for ten reais for half an hour."

"That's great, man, thanks."

I guzzled the rest of my water, followed by the cafezinho, then realized João still wasn't finished.

"Mike, do you really need to use the Internet?"

"Yeah, why?"

He looked a little uncomfortable.

"Well, you had a beautiful woman here this morning. Isn't that better than the Internet?"

I finally understood his point.

"Yes, João, a beautiful woman is always better than the Internet, but in this case I really do need to do some research. I'm not going to be surfing for pornography."

He nodded his head like he finally understood my point.

"Oooh, please excuse me. When I heard you say Internet, I naturally assumed that…"

"Yeah, I know and it wouldn't have been the first time if I had actually been trying to see some pictures of naked women, but like I said, this time it's strictly for some information."

"And what about that woman you were with?"

"Ah, there's not much to say except that if you ever see me with her again, remind me that I shouldn't let her leave."

"That is too bad, my friend, but I will remind you."

"Thanks for the help, João."

CHAPER 22

THREE MINUTES LATER I walked in the door of the Café Internet Baiano. It was a chic little place, all of whose customers either had dreadlocks or some kind of face piercing. I raised the average age of the clientele by five years by walking in the door. João's estimated pricing was on the mark and in ten quick reais, I had myself another cafezinho and a laptop with a view of Chile Street.

I googled "racist groups in Brazil" and half a sip later I had some info. It was the same story as everywhere else in the world, a bunch of dimwits who had shaved their heads and decided that the cause of all their problems were people different from them. Jews, of course, were on the list as were blacks, homosexuals and people from the Northeast of Brazil. This was something new for me. In the United States we usually keep our irrational hate simple by focusing on the easily identifiable characteristics like skin color and maybe language. To randomly choose an entire geographic section of your own country to hate spoke of a sophistication of hatred that I didn't think anybody could pull off, with the possible exception of Parisians. Apparently the Northeasterners' primary misdeed was migrating from their impoverished, waterless region to the big cities to look for work. It sounded like a serious offense to me.

The two main groups were Carecas do Suburbio and Carecas do ABC. The first translated as Skinheads of the Suburbs, while the second meant ABC Skinheads, the ABC standing for three of the main industrial suburbs of São Paulo. Both groups were headquartered in São Paulo and appeared to limit their activities to that particular urban area in the south of the country. Their favorite activities were typical of what I knew about neo-nazi groups: assaults, harassment, robbery and drinking, most of it while listening to hardcore skinhead music.

While they sounded like a fun group of guys, their parties seemed to take place mostly in the south of Brazil. Salvador was probably a tough market for skinheads, given the low demand for organized racism in a city where the overwhelming majority of the residents were black. I tried searching for racist groups in Salvador, Brazil and came up empty-handed, except for a reference to Carecas do Suburbio. Since I had still had a little coffee left, I clicked on the reference just for the hell of it. What I got was an address for the group in Salvador. The logo, a shiny bald head with a pissed-off expression, was the same as on the home website in São Paulo. There was no phone number, but the address was 137 Palmeiras Street in the neighborhood of Barra in Salvador. I wasn't real sure where that was, but I figured Anjo could put me on the trail pretty easily. I jotted down the address, drained my cafezinho and stepped out into the street, feeling pretty satisfied with my bad self.

The self-satisfaction lasted all of ninety seconds. As I turned right to go back to the hotel, I noticed an uncomfortably familiar black sedan holding up the back ends of two of the four cops that had been watching Nelson's jogo do bicho operation earlier in the afternoon. I thought about ducking back into the Internet café, but decided against it since both of the cops had already seen me and were calling inside the door of the Hotel do Chile. The object of their yelling then stepped out into the street. Delegado Neto didn't look angry, but his smile was far from friendly. He extended his hand to me with Detective Santos close behind.

"Mr. Breza, so good to see you again."

There was no choice but to respond in kind.

"The pleasure is all mine, Delegado Neto, the pleasure is all mine."

We shook hands and both of us knew the other was lying. I nodded at Santos, who returned the gesture.

"What can I do for you Delegado Neto?"

"I was hoping, Mr. Breza, that you might be able to give me a moment of your time."

"I'm happy to cooperate with you in any way I can."

I almost pulled a muscle in my cheek trying to match his forced smile.

"Thank you, Mr. Breza. I need to ask what you know about the jogo do bicho here in Brazil."

I didn't like the sound of the topic of conversation, but it didn't seem like I could request another category. I stalled, thankfully without stammering.

"The jogo do bicho?"

"Yes, the jogo do bicho. What do you know about it?"

I was waiting for inspiration to arrive, but apparently the idea bus was running late. I decided to come clean.

"What I think I know is that the jogo do bicho is like a big lottery in which people pick certain animals and bet that those animals will be picked in a drawing that takes place three times daily. If the animal you chose gets drawn, then you can win some money. That's what I think I know."

"Did you know that the jogo do bicho is illegal?"

The answer to that question was pretty obvious.

"Illegal? Are you kidding? Everybody plays it. How can it be illegal?"

"It is illegal because Brazilian federal law makes it so. And my information is that not only have you played twice since you arrived here in Salvador, you have won both times. And by playing the same bet both times. Do you know how difficult this is?"

"No, I really don't. Is it unusual?"

My ability to keep a straight face was strained to the breaking point with that whopper.

"It is unusual enough to get the attention of the federal police and raise questions about what relationships you might have with the bicheiros here in Salvador."

"What's a bicheiro?"

"A bicheiro is someone involved in running the jogo do bicho. How much money did you win?"

"Four hundred and fifty reais."

"Where is it?"

"The money?"

"Yes, where is it?"

"It's gone. I bought some beer for the corner boys, some lunch for my cousin and I gave the rest away."

"You gave the rest away? To who?"

Delegado Neto wasn't going to be very happy if I told him about the widows of the murder victims, so I stayed very general.

"Just people less fortunate than me."

Delegado Neto gave me a first class tough guy stare. Then he put his hand on my shoulder and leaned in close so he could talk in a low voice that I'd still be able to hear. Santos leaned in as well.

"Mr. Breza, there will not be anyone less fortunate than you if you do not stay away from the jogo do bicho here in Salvador. It is a highly illegal activity and I have been charged with cleaning it up. I intend to accomplish this goal and I plan to be ruthless in achieving it. If you continue to play or if you associate with the people who run the game, the bicheiros, you will find yourself in a very ugly situation with the federal police. Is that clear?"

Even for a man of my limited intellect, it was pretty clear.

"Delegado Neto, I will absolutely stay away from the jogo do bicho. Thank you for informing me."

"It is my pleasure."

His smarmy smile told it would be his even greater pleasure to slap some bracelets on me and stuff my head in the nearest prison toilet. He, Santos and the muscle climbed in the sedan and pulled away, leaving me in front of the hotel entrance.

João stuck his head out. He looked both ways before motioning for me to come in.

"Oy, Mike, what was that all about? Do you know who that was?"

"Unfortunately I do know who that was. Delegado Neto of the federal police. I'm not sure of his first name."

"Some people say it's Antonio, but I've never heard anybody call him anything but Delegado. What did he want with you?"

"Well, he wanted to talk about my winning the jogo do bicho a second time."

"Yeah, that's some luck, man."

The black sedan faded into the afternoon traffic.

"I'm not so sure, João. I'm not so sure."

Chapter 23

It was about six o'clock and I didn't feel like flopping around in my hotel room, so I headed down to the docks for some family togetherness. I felt like a pro on the Lacerda Elevator and the operator was the same one as the first time I'd used it. He seemed a little disappointed that I gave him some Brazilian coins instead of a U.S. greenback, but gave me a smile anyway. Bones was standing on the dock looking at his boat when I got there.

"Hey, Mike, down here so soon? What's the matter? You couldn't find any more government officials to piss off in the upper city?"

"Actually, you're right, so I pissed off the same one again."

He threw his head back and laughed, then saw that I was serious.

"Aw, fuck me, Mike, what happened?"

I told him everything about my second run-in with Delegado Neto. That led to a lot of head-shaking.

"Mike, you've got to be careful. The federal police here in Brazil are not to be trifled with."

"I think it's safe to say that my jogo do bicho days are over."

"I'll miss the high life we were leading, but it's probably for the best."

We climbed on board to watch the day fade away with a beer and had just settled down with our backs to the dock when some kind of commotion broke out behind us. There was a crowd gathered around some kind of late afternoon entertainment that turned out to be two guys brawling. By the time we got to the circle of spectators, it had degenerated into a wrestling match between a white middleweight and one of the flyweight dock guys that kept an eye on Bones' boat. In spite of the weight differential, the match looked pretty even with the flyweight giving as good as he was getting. When both parties looked too exhausted to be worth any more of the crowd's time, two of the other dock guys pulled them apart. Both of their shirts were ripped, the white guy had blood dripping from his chin and the dock guy's left eye was starting to swell. It looked like a nice amateur dust-up. The white guy was about five feet from us when he called the dock guy a son-of-a-bitch in Portuguese and spit in his direction. He then spun on his heel and walked away with a slight limp. The dock guy responded with a slightly different insult directed at the white guy's mother and the crowd dispersed. I looked over at Bones.

"Not bad for cheap entertainment."

He kept looking at the white guy walking away.

"Bones, what's up?"

"I know that guy from somewhere. I've seen him before."

"Well, you've been parked at this dock for how long now, two weeks? He's probably just another salty dog you've seen hanging around the beautiful people yachts like yours."

"Nah, that's not it. He's not from the docks. I'd know it if he was."

"So then where do you know him from?"

He shook his head to clear out the cobwebs, but to no avail.

"It'll come to me."

"I don't know about that, but I can tell you that something else is coming."

The rhythmic beep of a tourist taxi pulled up way too close to both of us, close enough to merit inspection of the driver by the dock boys. Of course they had nothing but smiles and embraces for Anjo as he stepped out of his cab. After satisfying this particular branch of his fan club, he came over to us in front of the Sweet St. Pete.

"Senhores Mike and Bones! Como vão?"

Even I could understand that question in Portuguese.

"It's all good, Anjo. How was the driving?"

He grinned and tapped a big wad of bills in his front pocket.

"I have been very successful this afternoon. I will pay for dinner tonight."

Bones wasn't in a mood to tolerate this.

"Dinner is on me tonight. You can buy us a beer if you want, but nothing more."

Anjo looked at me to see if it was worth his while to protest, but I shook my head. He went along.

"Then I invite you both to a very cold beer. There is a very excellent place to drink it over on the Rua Portugal and a delicious and inexpensive restaurant on the same street."

He didn't have to repeat himself.

As we crossed the Cayru Plaza, I heard my name being called. It was Wanda Miranda, working the lower level of the Modelo Market. She abandoned a group of at least four potential diners to come over and speak to us.

"Oy, Mike Breza, voce e muito generoso!"

The only thing I understood was my name, and that was a triumph in and of itself. Anjo could tell from the look on my face.

"She says you are very generous, Mike."

"Why's she saying that?"

Wanda was on top of us as I asked.

"I say it because it is true. You give two hundred fifty reais to three women you not know."

"How did you hear about that?"

She looked at me and shrugged.

"People talk."

I was beginning to feel like people in Salvador didn't talk about anything else besides me, but since it was all pretty good press, I didn't see much reason to get agitated. Wanda gave me a big kiss on the cheek. With two kisses in one day, I was doing much better in Brazil than I ever did on a normal day in Manhattan.

"Thank you, Wanda."

She gave us a smile and headed back to hustle up diners for Camafeu de Oxossi. We kept walking over to

Portugal Street, where Anjo led us into another hole-in-the-wall called A Caverna. It was about as well-lit as the cave it was named for, but the food was delicious and the beer was ice cold. Since Anjo ordered for us, we had some kind of fish soup with plenty of coconut that was apparently a specialty of the house. Anjo regaled us with a couple of stories about his fares for the day and I countered with a brief description of my afternoon chat with Delegado Neto. With that the mood got somber in a hurry.

"Oy, Mike, this is very serious. We must be careful not to get Delegado Neto more angry than he already is. If he came looking for you at the hotel, he is not happy with you and wants you to know it."

"Yeah, his tone sort of gave me that idea. That and his threat about how nobody in Salvador would be less fortunate than me if I didn't stay away from the jogo do bicho."

We all agreed that avoiding Nelson for a day or so might be a good way to lower our profile. At that point, I told my partners about my Internet adventure. Both of them were surprised to hear of an organized hate group with an address in Salvador. Anjo had heard stories about official racist groups in São Paulo and Porto Alegre, the capital of the southernmost state in Brazil, but couldn't get his mind around the concept of an organized racist group in Salvador.

"Someone with that much hate must be very tired all the time with all the hating he has to do in this city."

"Look, I agree with you, but we have to go check the address out. With a nice little swastika carved into each victim's back, a bunch of neo-nazi skinheads looks like a pretty good lead to me. Do you know where 137 Palmeiras Street is, Anj?"

He was pretty insulted that I seemed to be doubting his taxi-driving Salvador street knowledge.

"I can drive you there blindfolded right now."

"I'll settle for tomorrow morning with both your eyes wide open. What time can we do it?"

"I will come for you at nine o'clock."

"Bones, any interest in coming along?"

"Nah, I'm gonna leave the early a.m. sleuthing to you guys. I have plenty to do here on my boat if it's actually going to make it back to Florida."

I would have given him some shit for his reply, but the sight of his reais landing on top of the bill convinced me to hold my tongue. We walked back to the docks, where Bones bid us good night. Then Anjo drove me up to the hotel. On the way he had a question for me.

"Mike, how do you feel about the investigation?"

It was a good question and I wished I had a better answer.

"To be honest with you, Anj, I'm not sure exactly how it's going right now. Even though it's only been a couple of days, the swastikas carved into the victims' backs make me think it's the same person or persons behind this and that it looks like what would be called a hate crime back in New York. But other than that, it seems a little early to classify our progess as good, bad or indifferent."

"The bad result with the police does not bother you?"

"Not as far as the case is concerned. It would have been nice if Delegado Neto had received us with cocktails and all the information his people had gathered on the case, but the truth of the matter is no police force in the world is going to reveal any information about a triple murder case to an unknown foreigner claiming to be a reporter. I had pretty low expectations about their cooperation, so I wasn't disappointed. What does bother me, though, is being associated with the jogo do bicho in Delegado Neto's mind. If he and his boys are watching us, we have mobility problems. That makes things a little more difficult."

"But you are not discouraged?"

"Not yet. Not as long as Delegado Neto doesn't ask me to wear shiny, inter-locking bracelets."

His grin told me my answers had satisfied him. We stopped in front of the Hotel do Chile and I opened the door.

"I will be here at nine o'clock, Mike."

"I'll be waiting, Anj."

With that he cut into traffic, pushed along by a swell of irate car horns.

CHAPTER 24

MY FIRST THOUGHT WAS that nine o'clock had shown up in a hurry, but my travel clock said it was only seven forty-five when I staggered out of bed to answer the knocking on my door. I was expecting either Anjo or an over-zealous maid, but I got something much different. I got something much better. It was Teresa Cardoso and she looked just as good as she had the day before in a pair of jeans with some kind of white blouse that contrasted with the deep ebony of her skin. Did all the women in Salvador look this good so early in the morning? Even if they didn't, it was a sure bet that the men couldn't look much worse than I did, standing in the doorway in a pair of ratty boxer shorts and a face full of morning stubble. I tried to remember if I'd brushed my teeth the night before, but it didn't matter because she practically tackled me while planting a huge kiss on my lips. Once I regained my balance, I had to unlock her arms from my neck and look for the words to ask her why in Portuguese.

"Porque voce e muito generoso."

I was flattered that she thought I was generous, but before my false modesty could rear its ugly head, she lip-locked me for a second time. Now something else was rearing its ugly head and there wasn't much I could do to stop it, not that I wanted to. I put my hands on her shoulders and ran them south to her hips. They felt just a good as they looked. I walked her over three steps and pushed the door shut. Then it was my turn to tackle her.

When the wrestling was over, I looked over at her stretched out on my bed while an earthquake coursed though my body. I told her as best as I could that I didn't have the words in Portuguese to say what I really wanted to say, so thank you would have to suffice. She smiled and asked me how to say thank you in English. I told her and she smiled again.

"Thank you, Mike Breza."

She went to the bathroom, then started to get dressed. I stopped her by wagging my finger and leading her to the bathroom again, where I filled the bathtub with the Hotel do Chile's special formula bubble bath. Teresa looked like she was getting a little antsy, so I told her that her job could wait five minutes. Then I made her get in the water. The look on her face was rivaled only by the one I'd seen about ten minutes earlier. I had a feeling that hot bubble baths were a little scarce in the favelas of Salvador. I cleaned her feet and her back, but left the rest for her to scrub. The five minutes turned to ten, but she was far from antsy when she got out of the tub. It seemed to me that the phrase "relaxed Brazilian" was a redundancy, but there was no other way to describe her. I toweled her down, then sat down to watch her get dressed. When she slipped on her second shoe, I took her hand. I pulled her close to me and whispered in her ear.

"Muito obrigado, Teresa Cardoso."

She kissed me again.

"Tchao, Mike Breza."

Then she was gone. It was eight forty-five. I jumped in the shower and when I came out, Anjo was sitting on the bed waiting for me.

"Bom dia, Mike."

"Bom dia, Anjo."

"You look tired, Mike. Did you sleep?"

"Yeah, of course. Why do you ask?"

He lifted his chin in the direction of the foot of the bed, where a used condom decorated the floor.

"I am not a detective, but some clues are too obvious to not see."

I surprised myself by wasting ten seconds trying to invent a believable lie before realizing that Anjo was unlikely to give a shit if I had gotten lucky with the sister of one of his constituents.

"That's from Teresa coming by to see me this morning."

"Teresa Cardoso?"

"That's the only Teresa I know here in Brazil."

"Nossa! You are a lucky man, Mike!"

"Yeah, well, she said I was a very generous man. It was a nice way to get paid back."

"I can tell you that all three women were very grateful, but I do not think the sisters of the other two will come here to thank you like that."

"That's probably a good thing since I've never been able to handle more than one woman at a time. As a matter of fact, I even have trouble with that."

"Most men would have trouble with Teresa Cardoso. She is a lot of woman for any man."

"I can confirm that, my friend. I only hope that the rest of the day is as good."

Anjo shook his head.

"Now that, Mike, will be very difficult."

By that time I had my clothes on, so we headed downstairs for some eggs and cafezinho in the spacious confines of the perpetually-deserted Hotel do Chile dining room. We somehow found a waiter and ordered our food. While we were waiting, João strolled in to wish us a good morning.

"Bom dia, senhores. Tudo bem?"

Since everything seemed all righter with me than with Anjo, I was the one to respond.

"Tudo bem, João, tudo bem."

He winked at the two of us.

"I saw your friend, Teresa, again this morning. Did you get a chance to, uh, talk with her?"

He knew damn well that not much talking had gone on.

"Yeah, we had a pretty good conversation."

"She looked very well-informed when she left the hotel. She had a knowledgeable smile on her face."

I gave him a knowledgeable smile of my own.

"Well, thanks for letting her come up, João. I assume you'll be phoning the local press with the news so the rest of Salvador can keep up with every single thing I do in this city."

"People will want photos. Do you have any?"

"Of course not."

"Do you want to buy some?"

The joke was older than I was, but that didn't stop João and Anjo from yukking it up. I had to admit it was a nice set-up. With that, our eggs arrived and João went back to the front desk. In between bites, I quizzed Anjo.

"How far away is Palmeiras Street from here?"

"Not very far. We can be there in fifteen minutes if the traffic is not heavy."

"And you've never heard about these guys, Carecas do Suburbio, here in Salvador?"

He shook his head.

"It still does not make sense. Almost everyone here in Salvador has African blood, whether they want to admit it or not. Who are these carecas going to hate unless they hate themselves, too?"

I didn't bother to tell him that there were miles of couches on West Ninth Street in Manhattan occupied by people suffering from that very affliction.

Twenty minutes later we were mired in traffic so thick that it seemed like the West Side Highway on a Friday afternoon in the summer. Anjo's use of the horn was impressive, but I felt that his cursing was a little subdued by New York standards. Still, he showed impressive jockeying ability by cutting down several side streets, mostly in the right direction, and got us to Palmeiras Street in just under half an hour. Number one thirty- seven was a private house surrounded by a brick wall with a white wrought iron gate. It looked somewhat pricey for a bunch of racist skinheads. Anjo rang the bell on the gate. Thirty seconds later, a dark-skinned, middle-aged maid answered the door. Anjo asked her if the house was the headquarters for a group called Carecas do Suburbio. This set her to scratching her head until a light went on inside.

"Deve ser coisa do filho Luiz."

She hollered out the kid's name like he was in some other city and sure enough, a minute later a skinny, white kid with a clean-shaven head appeared at the gate. He looked about fourteen years old and I thought we might have had something of substance until his two equally skinny, equally cue-ball buddies trailed into the frame behind him. They had a hairstyle in common with Luiz, but the similarity ended there. They were both the same deep shade of black as Anjo. My razor-sharp detective instincts, honed by years in the business, led me to turn to Anjo, who was also looking at me.

"Anj, something here doesn't add up."

Anjo called over the three kids over to introduce himself. He explained that we were looking for a racist group by the name of Carecas Do Suburbio and that a website had given this address on Palmeiras Street. The three skinheads got a big laugh out of that. All of them launched into a simultaneous explanation that would have been a mystery for me if it hadn't been for the skilled air guitar, drums and bass that the three of them mimed for emphasis. In the midst of the chattering, Anjo turned to me.

"Carecas Do Suburbio is the name of their band."

"Don't tell me, Anj, let me guess. They play punk rock, right? Punk rock, right guys?"

They didn't speak English, but they all understood the term well enough to shout it back at me with a level of enthusiasm only fourteen-year-old Ramones fans could muster. I led them in a chorus of "Hey, ho, let's go" while Anjo stared at me in disbelief. They were still singing and bouncing like pogo sticks as we walked back to Anjo's taxi. Once we were safely seated where the seat belts should have been, Anjo looked at me with a twisted grin.

"Mike, as I heard you say more than once in New York, what the fuck was that?"

It required a longer answer than he really wanted to hear. I gave him the abridged version.

"It's cultural imperialism in the service of too much testosterone, Anjo. They're a bunch of kids trying to be punk rockers without the haircuts. My guess is the shaved heads drive their parents crazy, at least in the case of the white kid."

"They mentioned that it was part of their look."

"Yeah, well, it's a look designed to make a fourteen year old's parents wonder where they went wrong. Did they say anything about the name Carecas Do Suburbio?"

"They just said that Luiz had seen the name in the paper and liked it. When they decided to shave their heads, they chose it for the name of their band. Then they put it on their own website on the Internet."

"And they stole the symbol from the real Carecas Do Suburbio, right?"

Anjo nodded.

"They thought it went well with their look."

"Well, at least it's a case of truth in advertising."

I didn't tell him what a waste of time the trip had been. He probably knew that already. I also didn't bother telling him that I wished I'd spent the rest of the morning in bed with Teresa Cardoso. But Anjo probably knew that, too.

CHAPTER 25

IT WAS AFTER TWELVE by the time we got back to the hotel and Anjo ditched me to go use his cab for something useful, like make some money. I figured the odds of Teresa Cardoso showing up at my hotel room in the middle of the day were pretty slim, so I started walking toward the Lacerda Elevator to go to the lower city. I wanted to see what Bones looked like doing physical labor on his boat. As I entered the small plaza surrounding the elevator, I saw Wanda Miranda on the left selling pastries and deserts. She was dealing with some clients, so I just yelled her name and waved as I walked by. Two steps later a little kid was tapping on my arm, telling me that Wanda wanted to speak to me. He practically took me by the hand to drag me over to her, so I couldn't refuse. Wanda's money-paying clients had dissipated by the time I got over to her makeshift table. She reached out and handed me a bag.

"Para voce, Mike."

I reached for my pocket and she slapped my hand.

"No pay! No pay!"

The fire in her eyes told me she meant it, so I took the bag. There were four pastries inside and they smelled like heaven. I decided I was too hungry to share all four with Bones, so I sat down on the bench next to Wanda's wares and took a bite. It was almost as good as what I'd had before breakfast. It was all I could do to keep from drooling on her.

"Wanda, what is this? O que e isto?"

She smiled at my Portuguese. I figured that anything less than a guffaw was a sign that I was improving.

"Isso e bolinho de estudante. Student cake."

"Whoever invented it should get an A in the class."

She smiled, either because she didn't understand my stupid joke or because she did and knew it was stupid. She passed me a bottle of water and I took a big gulp to wash down every last crumb. It took all of my willpower to refrain from stuffing the other three pastries in my mouth. Wanda passed me a napkin and I cleaned up as best I could. When I finished, she was ready with a question.

"Como vai o seu caso? How your case goes?"

I didn't want to lie too much, so I told her it was going more or less well. She looked at me like she didn't really believe me, but she kept it to herself. Then she leaned over to speak to me in a low voice.

"When you have problem, talk with me."

"What kind of problem?"

"Any problem."

"How about women problems?"

She had a knowing look in her eye.

"No, I cannot help you with Teresa Cardoso."

At that point I really had no right to be surprised by anyone in Salvador knowing my personal business, but this gossip wasn't even five hours old. The sheets in my bed were still warm and Wanda Miranda was already in the know. I had half a mind to go back to the Café Internet Baiano to see if somebody had posted a video online. But what the hell did I care? I focused on my Portuguese pronunciation for Wanda's sake.

"Teresa Cardoso não e um problema para mim."

I could still hear her laughter when the elevator doors closed.

CHAPTER 26

BONES WAS SWEATING LIKE an ox when I found him doing something or another on his deck. I couldn't tell what it was he was doing, but since it involved tools and manual labor, I knew that I didn't want to get too close. I tried to steer the conversation toward a more social subject.

"Ahoy, Cap'n Bones, is there any beer aboard?"

I managed to duck just in time to avoid being hit by a piece of wood.

"If you don't knock off the ahoy shit, next time I won't miss you. I swear it!"

I'd forgotten how sensitive he was to nautical slights.

"Okay, okay, I'll stick to my landlubber vocabulary."

"That's exactly the problem, you moron. There's nothing more landlubber than the phrase "Ahoy, Cap'n". Except maybe "Ahoy, matey", which I believe you've already abused once here in Salvador."

By this time I'd gotten close enough to Bones to see that the real source of his frustration was a deck nail he was struggling to remove. Growing up, Bones was never one to admit the true reason he was pissed off, especially when it was so easy and convenient to lay it all off on the first person who spoke to him. Everybody in the family knew this about him, except, of course, him. I leaned over his shoulder to get a better look at the nail.

"You need me to pull that out for you? You know, so you can stop yelling at me?"

"My yelling at you has nothing to do with this fuckin' nail!"

"Uh-huh."

"Hey, it doesn't!"

"Just the same, you want me to yank it for you? We'll both feel better."

He rolled his eyes, shook his head and handed me the hammer. A minute later we were both sitting in the shade with a beer. Bones' day had taken a turn for the better. He clinked my bottle with his.

"Hey, thanks for the help with that nail, Mikey."

"My pleasure, man."

"But don't ahoy me anymore, all right?"

"Lesson learned."

"How come you're not with Anjo?"

"Ah, the skinhead lead turned to shit."

"How so?"

"It was a bunch of kids with a punk music band rebelling against their parents. Two of them were black."

"I guess that eliminates the racist angle there."

"Pretty much, yeah."

Bones snapped to attention.

"Hey, speaking of racism, I remembered where I knew that guy from."

"What guy is that?"

"You know, the white dude who got into a fight over here on the docks the other day."

"Okay, so where's he from?"

"He's from the deep south somewhere. Alabama or Mississippi."

"Whoa! You know this guy from somewhere in Alabama?"

"I don't know him, I just know who he is."

"Okay, I give up. Who's on first?"

"His name is Raymond Beecher and he was involved with some kind of neo-Ku Klux Klan group."

"A neo-Ku Klux Klan group?"

"Yeah, they hated all the same people as the original KKK, but drew the line at lynching. They just wanted to get all non-white people out of their neighborhood."

"So what happened?"

"Well, they weren't into lynching, but property damage was a main part of their strategy. They'd burn crosses, post threatening signs, that sort of thing."

"Did he get ever get busted?"

"Yeah, he got nailed for conspiracy to destroy some black family's house and got shipped off to do ten years. It was a huge deal at the time, all over the papers down south."

"Are you sure about that?"

"I'm sure about Raymond Beecher's story and I'm also pretty sure that was him on the dock the other day."

"What would he be doing here in Brazil?"

"Speculation is more a part of your job description, Mr. Detective, not mine. But I will tell you this much. Back in the day when Mr. Beecher was a professional deep south racist, one of his group's favorite symbols was the bent cross itself."

"The swastika?"

"The very same, my friend."

I put my half-full bottle down and stood up. Bones seemed surprised.

"Hey, where are you goin'? I've got some more nails for you to pull."

"Not today, Cuz. You just put me back in the mood to work. Thanks for the inspiration."

"So where are you going?"

"Back up to my favorite Internet café to google one Mister Raymond Beecher."

CHAPTER 27

RAYMOND BEECHER CERTAINLY HAD a big chunk of his personal story floating around in cyberspace. Date of birth, hometown, relationship with his parents, high school, his rapid rise in the underworld of hate groups; it was all there. He was a bit of a firebrand in his twenties, always anxious for a soapbox to climb on, always ready to spew some hate. His group was called WhiteFirst! and at its peak it had just north of a couple thousand members. The conspiracy charge he was locked up for stemmed from being caught outside an African American family's house at night with lots of full gasoline cans, matches and a wooden cross in his trunk. The FBI also managed to tie him to some threatening letters the family had received about some kind of cross that was going to burn on their lawn if they didn't pack up and move out lickety-split. It turned out that the only thing lickety-split about the affair was the speed of his trial, conviction and disappearance from view. One website had a rumors page that talked about how he had been spotted all over the world since his release from prison a couple of years ago. About the only country not on the list was Brazil. According to the rumors, he was responsible for racial unrest in Africa, Europe, the Philippines, everywhere but the United States and South America. By the looks of it, the man got around, even after serving a solid ten-year sentence.

The most recent photo I found bore some resemblance to the late-thirties, white brawler I had seen on the dock, but the quality of the reproduction on the screen was somewhat less than top-notch. Not to mention that the guy on the docks had exhibited a full head of graying hair, unlike the sneering skinhead that stared out at me from the computer screen. One detail that didn't escape me was that Beecher had a tattoo of a swastika on his chest. That might've helped me with confirming that the white guy in the fight was Beecher, but I needed to go back to the docks to speak with the flyweight that had slugged it out with my would-be bad guy to find out if he knew where his sparring partner lived.

I turned right as I stepped out of the door and the same big, black sedan was parked in front of the Hotel do Chile. This time, however, Delegado Neto was nowhere in sight. The main car-leaner was Detective Santos. He looked a little less like a young deer in the headlights, but he would still need some solid ID to get served at any place where I was tending bar. He nodded at me as I walked by, so I did the same to him. I was happy to have a police encounter in which nobody got yelled at. On my way back to the Lacerda Elevator, I exchanged waves and smiles with Wanda Miranda.

Bones was still struggling with minor boat repairs when I got back, but it looked like a couple of beers had taken the edge off his frustration. He saw me coming.

"Don't say it, Cuz. Just don't say it. I have a beer bottle here and I'm not afraid to use it."

"I'll keep my landlubber comments to myself."

"In that case, come aboard."

We sat down in the same shade as before with different beers.

"So what did you find out?"

"It was like you said. This guy Raymond Beecher was some kind of racist skinhead that got popped and wound up doing ten years in one of the nation's most luxurious federal facilities."

"I told you so."

"Yeah, well, now I have to find out if the guy we saw brawling on the dock is in fact Raymond Beecher. Do you know the guy that was fighting with him?"

Bones shook his head.

"Nah, but somebody over here will know who he is. They might even know who the white guy was. Let's take them some beers."

We each grabbed three beers and walked over to where the dock boys were hanging out. After some thanks on their part and a few questions on what animal was the most likely to win the next jogo do bicho, Bones broke out his seafaring Portuguese to ask about the fight. Nobody knew the white guy, although they'd seen him around, but the black guy was another story. His name was Otavio and he was a cousin of the ringleader of the docks, a muscular black man named Jose. Jose told us his cousin was still growing, but could hold his own in a street fight. Jose was obviously very proud of that fact. Otavio apparently had no fixed address, just a bunch of girlfriends that could put him up from time to time. Other nights he slept on the docks with the boys. There was no doubt that sooner or later Otavio would turn up, but the timing was pretty fluid. Bones asked the guys to let him know when Otavio showed and we left them with their beers and a nice sunset in their future. The shade was still the place for us to be.

We'd barely parked our butts back in that shade when Anjo's taxi came into view. By the size of his grin, I guessed he'd had a very successful afternoon.

"Oy, senhores! Como vão?"

He bounded onto the boat like a man with money in his pocket and Bones offered him a beer. I filled him in on how Raymond Beecher had moved into our spotlight. Anjo couldn't believe his ears.

"This man was in jail for trying to hurt black people?"

I nodded.

"But he hadn't hurt them yet?"

"No, but he had a pretty long history of trying to do so. Why?"

"In Brazil the hurt would have to be done for anybody to go to jail, especially if it was a black person being hurt."

He shook his head.

"It is quite a system of justice you have in the U.S.A."

Since there was no reason to disillusion him, I changed the subject to Otavio.

"So Anjo, do you have any idea of where we can find Otavio?"

Anjo shook his head.

"If his cousin, Jose, doesn't know, then there is only one other person who can help you."

"And who might that be?"

Anjo gave me his I-Can't-Believe-You-Don't-Know-This face.

"Mike, who could it be?"

"I don't know. Shango?"

"I said a person, not an orixa."

I was out of guesses.

"Wanda Miranda, Mike, Wanda Miranda."

That made sense since she seemed to know everything about what I was doing in Salvador. Why shouldn't she keep tabs on the rest of the city's population?

"So I should ask her if she knows where to find Otavio?"

"You should tell her which Otavio you want to find."

"And she'll just tell me?"

"Probably not, but she will help you."

"How?"

"It is impossible to predict how, but I guarantee you that she will help"

My legs didn't want to do it, but I stood up anyway.

"Okay then, let's go talk to her. She's in the plaza by the Lacerda Elevator selling her pastries."

My cohorts fell in behind me and we made for the elevator. It was about four o'clock, so I didn't think she'd be wrangling customers for Camafeu de Oxossi at that hour. Sure enough, when we got upstairs she was still in the same place. The only thing that had changed was that her pastry board was sparsely populated at best. Anjo called out to her and she responded in kind.

"Kawo-kabyesile."

"Kawo-kabyesile."

They hugged each other. Then Wanda turned to me.

"Seu Mike Breza. Aqui de novo? Back again?"

"Always, Wanda, always."

Bones elbowed me.

"Oh, Wanda, this is my cousin, Bones."

Bones extended his hand.

"Muito prazer."

Wanda took his hand, but looked at him with a question in her eye.

"Your name Bones? Ossos?"

"Ah, it's a nickname. My real name is Gary."

Wanda nodded.

"Bones e melhor. Bones better."

We all knew she was right. It was my turn to chime in.

"Wanda, I now have a problem that I need your help with."

She smiled like she knew it all along. Anjo then explained about the brawl and that we were looking for Jose's cousin, Otavio. At that point, Wanda interrupted.

"Otavio skinny, no?"

I wanted to contribute a little to the conversation.

"Like a pencil."

"And very dark, no?"

"Very dark, yes."

"And young?"

"Yeah, he's pretty much a kid."

"He wear blue Bermudas and white shirt?"

I had a bad feeling that my mouth was hanging open because I didn't know the answer. I snuck a look at my buddies and their expressions were no more intelligent than mine.

"Uuuuuh, I don't know. Do you guys know?"

They didn't know either, so Wanda asked again.

"He wear green Havaiana sandals?"

I didn't even bother with the "uuuuuh".

"I, that is, we, don't know."

"Then you must find out."

"How do we do that?"

"You look over there."

She pointed across the plaza on the other side of the elevator. There was a skinny, dark kid dressed just as she had described him. It was Otavio. He was parked on a bench next to a girl of about the same age. The two of them were laughing and eating what looked like some of Wanda's wares. I looked at Anjo. He gave me a half-smile that was the loudest I-told-you-so I'd ever been subjected to. I couldn't contain myself. I looked around at Wanda and tried to keep the disbelief in my voice to a minimum.

"How did you know he was there, Wanda?"

This time she acted surprised at the question.

"He buy my student cakes right now, just like you. Then he go over there with his girl to eat. I see him, so I know."

It didn't really matter if it was orixa energy, coincidence or plain, old dumb luck; we'd found our guy. I bought a round of student cakes for all of us and paid Wanda double. Then we strolled across the plaza to where Otavio was smiling at his girlfriend of the moment.

Otavio's smile got even broader when he saw Anjo. He stood up to shake all of our hands and introduced his girlfriend, Josefina. Anjo told him the part of our story that Otavio needed to know, namely that we'd seen him fighting with some white guy on the docks that we needed to talk to. Otavio nodded and said he only knew the guy well enough to say that he never wanted to get into another dispute with him over whose turn it was on the pool table at any bar in the city. He confessed to having jumped the line at a bar called A Encruzilhada a few days before the brawl and his sparring partner had called him on it. The next time the white guy saw him, the two of them exchanged words and we had seen the tail-end of the result. Then Anjo asked for the guy's name. Otavio shrugged.

"Raimundo."

Bones whispered in my untrained ear.

"That's Raymond for those of you keeping score at home."

Otavio sort of knew where Raimundo lived. It turned out to be João de Deus Street, on the way to the Pelourinho. The bar where the initial dispute between Otavio and Beecher had taken place was on the same street. Otavio thought the regulars might be able to give us Raimundo's exact address. Through Anjo I asked if there was anything else about the guy that he could tell us. His answer came in a Portuguese that I couldn't decipher, so I turned to Anjo. He looked a bit puzzled.

"So what did he say, Anjo?"

Anjo waited a couple of seconds before answering me.

"Otavio says that in spite of the fight, in his opinion, Raimundo is actually a nice guy. They've played pool together many times."

I didn't tell him that everybody's nice on the surface. You have to drill a little deeper to see the real personality. I wasn't too sure about how deep I'd have to go, but I was willing to bet that Raymond Beecher was different on the inside. He had the track record to prove it.

CHAPTER 28

IT WAS PRETTY EASY to get where we were going. Hell, I felt like I could've done it even without Anjo as my guide, but I wasn't yet foolish enough to try. We crossed the Praça da Se, passed the cathedral again and took a right to find ourselves on João de Deus Street. We tracked down A Encuzilhada on the corner of João de Deus and Juiz C. Rabelo Streets. It was pretty easy to spot, what with the picture of a smiling devil standing at the intersection of two paths painted in red and black on the door. When we stepped inside, there was a table on the right with a statue of a small, black chicken resting on it. Next to it was an empty bottle of cachaça and an empty jar of honey. I had managed to forget most of what Anjo had taught me on his excellent New York adventure about Candomble, but I knew a special offering when I saw it. I put a couple of reais on the table and I looked over at Anjo.

"Hey, Anj, this looks like a hangout for Exu."

He gave me a broad smile.

"You remember, Mike. That is good."

It was hard to forget, considering that Exu had been instrumental in saving our lives back in New York. Exu was an orixa, an African deity, or something close to it, that had stowed away in the mental baggage of the Yoruba slaves brought over to Brazil to be worked to death. The rules of Candomble said that Exu frequented the crossroads and that to communicate with the other fifteen orixas, you had to get Exu's help first. I started to think that the Encruzilhada might be just the place for us, since we needed all the help we could get.

Compared to the Amor Cego, the Encruzilhada was as solid as Fort Knox. It was a big open room with brick walls, a solid wooden bar lined with stools opposite the door and a few tables scattered around the room. The three pool tables were obviously the big attraction and they were all in use when we walked in. Anjo got a couple of waves and at least one bear hug, but nobody put their eyes on Bones and me for more than a nanosecond. That was all it took for them to check us out and classify us by the time we reached the bar. Since we didn't look like either hustlers or marks, everybody lost interest and turned their attention back to the action on the tables. Anjo called the barkeep over. I started to ask him a question, but Anjo shushed me.

"First we act like customers."

I felt pretty silly, having violated a cardinal rule of being in a bar. Anjo asked for three beers. I reached for my pocket, but he grabbed my wrist.

"I will pay, Mike. It was a good afternoon of work."

The bartender was a chatty type and got chattier once he collected Anjo's money. He knew exactly who we were talking about when Anjo described him. Actually, he knew who it was as soon as Anjo used the adjective "white". It turned out that Raimundo Bicher, as everybody at the bar knew him, did not, in fact, live on João de Deus Street. He lived around the corner at 66 Juiz C. Rabelo Street, a couple of doors down from the bar. His was the apartment, if you could call it that, on the second floor. We left the barkeep in mid-sentence with only our half-full beers as company.

As we made the right-hand turn onto Juiz C. Rabelo, I ran through the scenario in my mind. I imagined we'd ask if he really was Raymond Beecher and get either a shocked look, a door slammed in our faces or both. We might be able to get another question in before picking splinters out of our noses, but that would probably be the extent of it. We'd have to stake him out, find out where he worked, what kind of operation he might be organizing in Brazil, who his colleagues were and what friends he had, if any. I had the full extent of the operation we were going to need completely mapped out in my head by the time we go to the second floor apartment. I told Anjo to knock and say he was from the bar on the corner, that we thought Raimundo might have left something behind. Anjo nodded his head in agreement and even Bones thought it was a good idea. After three light knocks on the door, a voice asked us in Portuguese who was there. Anjo spun his yarn and the sound of footsteps tap-tapped up to the door, which swung open without the sound of locks being undone, revealing the absolute last thing any of us had ever expected to see.

CHAPTER 29

IT WAS A BLACK woman. She was probably in her thirties and had a tight afro that made her gold hoop earrings seem even larger than they were. She was barefoot, pretty and waiting for us to say something. Fortunately Bones recovered from his surprise enough to croak out a question.

"Raimundo?"

This snapped Anjo out of his surprise enough to follow up Bones' croaking with a very unconvincing explanation of how we thought maybe Raimundo had left something at the bar and could we possibly talk with him for a second if it wasn't too much trouble. Hearing it out loud made me wonder who could've come up with such a stupid sounding explanation. The woman probably thought the same thing because she gave us a strange look, then called back into the apartment.

"Meu bem, tem aqui um pessoal do bar que esta te procurando."

Even a linguistic ignoramus like me couldn't miss the use of "meu bem", a term of endearment between spouses or longtime lovers. Even more obvious was the "meu amor" that Raimundo used when his hand posed lightly on the woman's shoulder as he appeared in the doorway. His squint told me that he didn't think we looked like we had come from A Encruzilhada, but he didn't say so. He was a little under six feet and probably weighed about one hundred seventy pounds, not very imposing for a southern-fried racist. There was a nice horizontal scar across his forehead that I hadn't seen in any of the photos on line. He kind of grinned and asked us what was up in Portuguese.

"O que e que ha, senhores?"

I was so flabbergasted that all I could think of to say was the obvious question.

"Are you Raymond Beecher?"

"I am."

"From Alabama?"

"The same."

Bones couldn't contain himself.

"Shit, I never expected to see you like this."

Beecher snorted without taking his eyes off us.

"Me neither. What can I do for you?"

I didn't feel like sucking on a mouthful of splinters, but I couldn't come up with a better story than the truth. I identified myself and told him exactly why the three of us were there. I told him about the bodies, but left out a lot of details he didn't need to know, giving him a five-minute summary in about thirty seconds. Then I laid my concluding sentence on him.

"Bones here recognized you in a fight on the docks the other day and, uh, given the nature of the crime..."

At that moment, Beecher held up his hand.

"Enough. I get the picture."

He gave a long, tired sigh.

"Look, give me two minutes to talk with Beatriz. I'll be right out."

No facial splinters resulted from his soft closing of the door. Ninety seconds later he came out.

"Let's go to the Encruzilhada. We can talk there."

We made no small talk on the way. When we got to the bar, the same barkeep teed up four beers. Beecher made it clear that we were paying. He took a sip and led us to a table in the darkest corner of the bar, away from the pool tables. We sat down and he looked at us for a second. Then he spoke.

"I thought I'd flown below radar on those murders."

I wasn't sure I understood.

"How so?"

"Come on, three black men turn up dead on the steps of a Catholic church with whip marks and swastikas carved into their backs. That's right, I saw them in the newspaper photos. Who's the first person you'd talk to? I don't know about you, but, me, I'd talk to the guy that has one of these tattooed on his chest."

With that, he unbuttoned his shirt and lifted a bandaid to show us a small swastika inside a circle tattooed right underneath his left breast. I had seen it in some photos, but it was different seeing it live and in person. None of us breathed a word. Beecher had to break the silence.

"For the record, I had nothing to do with the murders. I'm off that racist shit now."

I wanted to say that I had already figured out that something in his life had changed and that his black wife or girlfriend had been my first clue. Fortunately, I kept my mouth shut. Unfortunately, Bones didn't.

"When did you stop being a racist?"

"Well, it's still a work in progress, but it's been a few years now."

One of my cousin's most salient features was his uncontrollable curiosity.

"So how did that happen?"

Beecher shrugged.

"Does it matter?"

Bones had a long string of dead cats in his past. I was hoping we weren't heading for another.

"You were a founding member of WhiteFirst!, a nationally-known racist group that didn't limit itself to words. You got thrown in jail because you were about to incinerate a cross on a black family's lawn, the only hate crime you ever did time for, but I'm guessing there were lots of others. How does a guy like you get religion outside of the First Aryan Church of Whitebread? Somehow, I think that might matter, yes!"

I was surprised at Bones' vehemence, but had to admit that I liked it. I just hoped it wouldn't start a brawl with an ex-con. We got lucky. Beecher's reaction was just to shake his head.

"I spent a year listening to that kind of shit in the states after I got out and that was the nicest stuff I heard. My skinhead ex-buddies had even worse to say. The simple truth of the matter is that ten years is a long time. Time enough to grow up. Maybe not all the way, but enough to start understanding some things a little better."

He took another sip of his beer and leaned across the table toward Bones.

"Do you know how many black people I actually knew before I went inside?"

We didn't.

"Zero. Not a one. The first black person I ever had any extensive contact with was my cellmate when I got to prison."

He must have noticed the look in my eyes, because he elaborated.

"Yeah, that's right. My cellmate was black. That wouldn't come as a surprise to anyone who knows anything about the Alabama penal system, but it wasn't the logical choice for a skinhead prick like me. In my case, the warden just hated my guts. He told me so when they brought me in. Went out of his way to do it, too. I was picking up my Department of Correction fashion wear, when in comes Warden Griggs just to tell me he thinks I'm the biggest scumbag he's ever had behind his walls. The biggest scumbag in a prison full of rapists, murderers and thieves. That was some honor."

Beecher chuckled and shook his head as he sipped his beer again. Before he finished his swallow, Anjo came at him with a question.

"Was the warden a black man?"

Beecher looked at him.

"No, but his wife was black. Some folks thought that was unusual, too. Griggs put me in a cell with a black man on a cellblock with no other white person in sight. The only white people I saw except for yard time were the guards. Griggs told me he did it just to make my time inside worse. Turns out he did me a favor. Benjamin Edwards was six-five and went about two-fifty. He might've had some fat on him somewhere, but I sure as hell never saw it. He could've broken me in half any time he felt like it, but he didn't. He could've made me his bitch, but he didn't do that, either. He started out ignoring me, then spoke to me only to curse me out and intimidate me, something he did quite well, I might add. He eventually wound up talking with me and giving me pretty good advice. He was a hell of a cribbage player, too."

It all sounded just a little too fairy tale for my taste.

"So you developed this miraculous bond with a black man while in prison and this cured you of your racism? Just like that?"

He nodded.

"Yeah, pretty much, if a six or seven year process is your idea of 'just like that'. I caught a lot of beatings my first couple of years inside. You might say my reputation had preceded me, so I was a target everywhere I went. I have to admit that I deserved some of them, but more than a few were tough to justify. Anyway, about five and a half years into my stay, I got into a fight with some guy over something stupid and I kicked his ass good. I turned to walk away and one of the guy's friends tried to shiv me. He had piss-poor aim and wound up slicing my forehead instead of sticking me in the eye. Man, it was like somebody lit my head on fire. Blood was spurting everywhere. I couldn't see a thing and I thought I was a dead man. I would've been, too, if Big Ben hadn't stepped between us. They told me later that he took the shiv from the guy's hand like a rattle from a baby and threw the guy against the wall so hard his teeth were flapping in the breeze. I still couldn't see, but there was nothing wrong with my hearing. He announced to everybody that the white boy was off limits unless there was a legitimate complaint and that any score would be settled one on one. Anybody that had a problem with that could speak to him later. Then he made two other guys help him carry me and the guy whose ass I'd just kicked to the infirmary."

The three of us sat there with our mouths open. After a few seconds, I felt some words drifting out of mine.

"Why'd he do that?"

"He said everybody deserved a chance to defend himself. He didn't like sneak attacks, not even on racist scum like me. Said he also figured I'd taken enough gratuitous beatings, that it was time to put everything on a level playing field."

He took another sip of his beer.

"Up to the day that happened, Big Ben and I had been getting along pretty well. Couldn't say we were friends exactly, but we had a pretty civil relationship, especially for a hard-core racist and a black man. And I guess I'd started to have my doubts about all that shit I used to say about mud people and white superiority. Then he saved my life and I couldn't think that way at all anymore. How could I? When I got out of the hospital, I asked him if there was anything I could do to thank him and he told me to forget about it. He didn't even want anything in return. I got him something anyway, a new cribbage board, and he acted like Santa Claus had come, thanking me like I'd done him some great favor. Course then he kicked my ass up and down that board almost every time we played, but you get the idea. We got to be friends, real friends. Little by little I started talking to some of the other brothers, too, and a lot of them were just regular folks. There were also some extremely dangerous motherfuckers in there, too, don't get me wrong, but most of them weren't so different from me. I still had to fight once in a while, but it was always over regular prison shit, not skin color. Anyway, by the time I got out, I had no use for WhiteFirst! anymore and they had no use for me. That was it."

He drained his beer and looked at Bones.

"How 'bout another?"

Bones gave him a few bills and Beecher went and bought another round, even though we weren't done with ours. He took a big pull on his second beer and looked us over.

"You still haven't asked me where I was the nights of the murders, but I'm gonna save you the trouble and tell you I don't remember. I'm not even sure of when they took place, but I am sure it wasn't me. I'm also pretty sure that no matter what the dates were, Beatriz will be able to tell you exactly where I was those nights and who I was with."

Anjo spoke up.

"You were with her, yes?"

Beecher nodded.

"Every night. If I'm lucky enough not to blow it, it's for keeps."

I'd been alive long enough to hear some pretty strange tales and I'd been a detective long enough to know that when it comes to strange, fiction is nothing compared to the truth. Beecher had delivered his story too straight for it to be a lie; he wasn't the guy we were looking for. I didn't really need to know anything else, but I did have a couple of felines of my own to put at risk.

"So how did you end up in Brazil, Beecher?"

"When I got out, I had nowhere to go. Everybody in the U.S. knew who I was and thought they knew what I stood for, except for my old buddies, who couldn't stand me 'cause they knew everything had changed. And believe me, these weren't guys you want to have mad at you. I couldn't stay in the country and I couldn't go anywhere I'd be recognized. I had to get gone, man. I had some money from before I went inside, so I bought a plane ticket to Brazil just to get out of sight for a while. Now that while is stretching out to almost two years."

"Any plans on going back?"

"Not if I can duck the immigration cops and not if Beatriz keeps me."

I looked across the table at Anjo and Bones. They were nodding their heads in agreement. We were done. I put my beer on the table.

"All right Raymond Beecher. Thanks for your time. We're sorry to have troubled you."

He gave me half a grin.

"Does this mean you believe me?"

"Yeah, it does."

"Well, all right. "

I stuck my hand out and he shook it without getting up. He did the same with Bones and Anjo. After all, he had half a beer to finish. And maybe some pool to play. We were halfway to the door when Bones doubled back and said something else to Beecher, who hesitated slightly before he answered. Bones looked pensive when he reached us at the door.

"So what did you ask him?"

"I asked him why he hadn't gotten that swastika tattoo removed from his chest."

"What'd he say?"

"He said he kept it so he wouldn't ever forget how he used to think. Because then he might forgive himself."

The red and black door of the bar banged shut behind us.

CHAPTER 30

As we strolled back through the Praça da Se, it occurred to me that not much in the case was working out, so I decided to have some fun with Anjo.

"Hey, Anjo, what's the story with our buddy, Exu? I thought he was going to be a little more helpful."

Anjo knew when his balls were being busted.

"Ah, Mike, if you really want Exu to help you, you must offer him something. Exu is not the orixa to do something for free."

"Come on, what about that two reais I left on the table?"

"I would say that you received two reais of help."

"How so? I still don't know who the murderer is."

"No, but for two reais you are at least sure of who he isn't."

He had me and we both knew it. Even Bones laughed. By that time we had reached the Lacerda Elevator. Bones was going down to the Sweet St. Pete to teach some more nails a lesson, Anjo was going to chase some more fares and I needed a shower.

It was about seven-thirty when I stepped into the hotel and it was starting to get dark. As usual, João was behind the front desk, ready, willing and able to dispense gossip on command.

"João, como vai, cara?"

He said nothing, but a woman's voice came from the sitting area next to the dining room.

"Nossa! Que bom portugues!"

My Portuguese was really no better than my attitude, but both stood a great chance of improving based on the source of the comment. It was Teresa Cardoso, seated with her back straight and her legs crossed at the ankles on the sitting room's sofa. I surprised myself with my attention to the details surrounding her. She was wearing the same jeans and blouse I'd seen that morning and the combination looked even better now. I must've done my stupid statue imitation longer than I thought because she felt compelled to speak again.

"Boa tarde, Mike Breza."

Even I knew the correct response to that greeting.

"Boa tarde, Teresa."

I went on to stammer that she looked great and I probably got most of it right because João gave me a big, Brazilian thumbs-up before discreetly retiring. Since it was next to never that a beautiful woman came looking for me once, let alone twice in one day, I wasn't sure about how to greet Teresa. Fortunately, she took care of that by standing up and kissing me on the lips as I came over to where she was seated. I tried to tell her again what a thrill her showing up in the morning had been for me, but halfway through my linguistic stumbling something better occurred to me. I asked her if she would like to have dinner with me. She got a little shy, but said yes, and I hoped I could remember how to get to the hole in the wall Anjo had taken us to on Rui Barbosa Street. Through nothing less than divine intervention, I managed to find my way there and make conversation at the same time. The walls were still mint green, the tables were still Formica and there was still a dearth of paying customers, but at least this time around I noticed that the place actually had a name. It was called O Rei, which translates to English as The King. For a second I was worried that Teresa would be a little disappointed in the quality of the surroundings, but she didn't flinch and even flashed an Anjo-quality smile as we sat down. We had the finest table, of course, meaning the one with the best view of the TV, but we both managed to keep our eyes off it. I let her handle the ordering and whatever it was that we ate was delicious. We both drank a couple of cold beers with our mystery meal and she had desert and a cafezinho. I passed on the rocket fuel since I wanted to sleep at some point that night.

I've had easier first date conversations, but none that were as enjoyable. I struggled with a couple of verbs in Portuguese and I'm almost positive I told her she had pretty eggs instead of eyes, but other than that things went better than I would have expected. My linguistic skill improved with every sip of beer, while her tolerance for my mistakes increased at the same rate. I managed to learn that she worked as a maid for a rich family in the

Barra area of the city and that the commute was about an hour and a half each way.

I tried to tell her I worked as a bartender in New York when I wasn't keeping the city safe from all kinds of nefarious criminal activity and she seemed to get it because she smiled in all the right places. I got into a little adjective and noun trouble when she asked me how I'd met Anjo. The real, in-depth answer that the question begged for was beyond my abilities, but I emptied all my cartridges to give her a general idea of how it had come about. She told me a little about her son and her sister, Maria. I got the impression that she had no other close family besides them. The linguistic hurdles combined with the thrill of sitting across the table from Teresa made the time fly and before I knew it, it was ten-thirty. It occurred to me that I'd better get her a cab so she could make it home in time to get up to go to work again the next day, so I threw my reais on the table like a big shot as we stepped out in the street. I tried to ask if I could get her a cab to take her home, but I didn't get a very happy response. She lifted her eyebrows, shrugged her shoulders and made a little sideways movement with her head that even I could see meant she wanted no part of that plan. When I tried to explain that I'd be happy to accompany her to make sure she got home okay, her look turned to one of disbelief. It was then that I finally figured out that she probably wanted to stay with me.

It was still a little too much good for me to get my brain around, so I asked her if that was what she had in mind. It wouldn't have been the first time my lack of social awareness had pissed off a woman, but the response was so good I wanted to ask the question again. She took one step towards me, put her hand behind my head and, just before she kissed me, said what then became my favorite phrase in Portuguese.

"Claro, meu bem."

CHAPTER 31

THERE WAS A POINT in the next few hours where the dream I was living shifted from awake to asleep, but it was beyond me to say when it took place. All I knew was that I wanted it to continue for as long as possible, with the phrase "claro, meu bem" softly repeating in my mind.

Thunderclaps on my hotel room door, accompanied by screeches from beyond the grave, brought dreamtime to an end and re-introduced me to the real world. It took me a second to get my bearings, but I figured out that answering the door would be a good start. João was the bearer of bad tidings. It was five in the morning, it was dark outside and Anjo was on his way to pick me up. Another body had turned up on the steps of the church on the Rua do Passo.

The news cleared out all my mental cobwebs in a flash and I started looking around for my clothes. I found them scattered about in various parts of the room, but I didn't have time to re-live how they got there. I explained the situation to Teresa as best I could while I dressed. She looked worried, but I told her not to sweat it and to go back to sleep until I got back. I kissed her forehead and said I'd be back quickly and that everything would be fine. I only wished I believed it.

By the time I got downstairs, Anjo was already waiting for me. He looked like he was running on pure adrenaline, which was how I felt, too. We started out walking in the direction of the Praça da Se as Anjo filled me in.

"I was home in bed when somebody started to knock my door."

It occurred to me that I had no idea where the man lived, even though I'd already been in Salvador for four days.

"It was a moleque, a kid, telling me that another body had been thrown on the church steps."

"Did you get a look at it?"

He shook his head. I noticed that we were now jogging.

"No, I came directly for you."

We were running now, down past the Largo do Pelourinho and onto Carmo Hill. I could see a crowd at the iron fence that enclosed the stairs leading up to the church. There were a couple of cops standing in front of the gates, but crowd control didn't look like their specialty. They looked like they were waiting for the real police to get there. People were milling around talking, smoking and staring. Everybody looked like they had just gotten out of bed, just like me. The deadbeat cops were the only official presence for kilometers, or so it seemed. From the back of the crowd I could see the body was naked, but

I couldn't make out any gory details. Somebody noticed Anjo and the crowd parted like he was Moses. Even the cops stepped aside. We walked right up to the fence to get a better look.

The body was male and about ten feet away from us on the other side of the fence. It had some open wounds that were hard to identify from where we stood, but looked to be either burns or scrapes. There was no mistaking the other wounds, however, the long, oozing ones on the body's back. This man had been whipped and whipped bad. I couldn't see his entire body, but I didn't have to. I knew there was a swastika carved there somewhere in the dark brown skin. It was impossible to tell exactly what the cause of death had been, but the twisted expression on the man's face told me it had been painful. There was something else about his face as well. I crouched down and peered through the bars. Then it hit me like a hammer between the eyes. I knew this guy. I looked up at Anjo and I saw that he knew, too. It was Nelson, the guy who had sold me the winning jogo do bicho tickets.

CHAPTER 32

AT THAT MOMENT I saw a couple of black sedans make a
noisy appearance at the back of the crowd. I straightened
up as quickly as I could without making it seem like I
was in a hurry and started to move along the fence. I
grabbed Anjo's arm and dragged him with me. He started
to protest, but I just pulled him harder, making my way
toward the outside of the crowd, then working my way
back toward Carmo Hill. Once we were at the back of the
crowd I turned around to get a better look at the people
that had gotten out of the two sedans. I put my finger
to my lips and pointed back down toward the gates we
had just left behind. Anjo looked and saw what I saw.
It was our good friend Delegado Neto and his shadow,
Detective Santos. There were a couple of other suits with
them as well, but the guy in charge was clearly Neto. The
resistance melted from Anjo's face. He was finally on my
wavelength. I pulled him toward me to whisper in his
ear.

"Anjo, I suggest we get out of here right now."

We took a couple of steps toward the street and I turned around to get a last look. Neto and the boys had opened the gate and were stepping through it toward the body. No doubt to get a better look at the details that would never make it into any police report.

Anjo and I retraced our previous steps at a slower pace. We didn't say a word until we hit the Praça da Se. Once we got there, Anjo sat on a bench and put his face in his hands. I sat next to him and put my hand on his shoulder. The city was starting to wake up and all I wanted to do was go back to "claro, meu bem". But I didn't.

"How long did you know Nelson?"

Anjo didn't answer. I didn't ask again. After a minute he took his face out of his hands.

"I knew Nelson from when I had five years. We grew up together."

"So how did he wind up in the jogo do bicho?"

"He was always, you know, fast. He spoke well and always looked for a good deal."

"You mean he was a hustler."

"Yes, that is it. He was a hustler. To be a cambista for the jogo do bicho, you have to be a hustler. You have to be smart and you have to be able to talk well."

"It probably doesn't hurt to be good with numbers either."

Anjo nodded his head.

"Nelson was always very good in mathematics."

"Did he have a family, anybody we should contact?"

Anjo shook his head.

"No, his parents are long dead."

"No wife?"

Anjo finally smiled.

"A wife? Nelson? No, he was too much of a hustler."

I was glad Anjo's dark mood had lifted, if only for a second, but I knew it wouldn't last. I also knew we had to talk with the other guys from Nelson's corner to find out if anybody knew what had happened. I mentioned this to Anjo and he nodded.

"We will talk to them, but they will not know anything."

"How can you be so sure?"

"Because if we can talk to them, they will still be alive and they will only still be alive if they do not know anything about this."

His logic was hard to argue with.

We made our way over to the corner of Das Vassouras Street, where the mood was somber. It was about seven o'clock in the morning, but at least six or seven guys were hanging out on the corner where Nelson had done business, all of them with their faces at half mast. I recognized most of them from the other day and I pulled Anjo directly over to where my favorite three, Jesse, Jose and Wilson, were seated. Anjo explained what we were doing and translated my questions for me, distributing hugs of condolence along the way. In addition to the unholy trinity, we spoke with a Jaime, an Alfonso and a Freddy, none of whom knew a thing about what had happened. Nelson had packed it in at about nine o'clock the previous night and had gone off to do his thing. Most of the guys assumed his thing involved at least one and maybe two women, but nobody knew where he had gone. They only knew what we knew, that Nelson had wound up on the church steps with a body full of dead. We thanked the guys and walked back toward the Hotel do Chile. I asked Anjo what he was going to do. He looked at me with the most tired eyes I'd ever seen.

"Mike, I think I will try to sleep a little. Then I have to work some this afternoon. I will come look for you in the early evening."

"We're going to need to search Nelson's apartment, you know."

He nodded at me.

"What time will you be back?"

"Six o'clock."

"All right, man, I'll be waiting."

We put our arms around each other for the man hug and he got into his illegally-parked taxi. Then I was alone in front of the Hotel do Chile at eight o'clock in the morning. I went inside.

I nodded at the dude behind the counter and headed upstairs feeling like shit. As I was fumbling in my pocket for the key, the door to room 412 swung wide open. There was Teresa, almost partially covered by some of a sheet, the near-whiteness of which contrasted with her dark skin in such a way that I almost forgot all that I'd just seen. I was surprised to see her still there and I asked if she had waited for me instead of going to work. Then she said it again.

"Claro, meu bem."

She extended her hand behind my head and my life got much more perfect than I deserved. It didn't last as long as I wanted, but there's nothing in this world that could.

CHAPTER 33

I WOKE UP WITH a start. It was eleven o'clock and Teresa was nowhere to be seen. That was okay. I laid back down, shut my eyes and I could see her as clear as day. I could see every inch of her body that I had already seen twice in less than twelve hours. But since I wasn't going to get the chance to touch her, it occurred to me that I needed a cold shower followed by a hot cafezinho. The downside of that course of action was that I was going to have to get out of bed.

It was easily noon by the time I made it down to the lobby and into the deserted dining area. I looked around, but there didn't seem to be anybody there. As usual, I underestimated the all-knowing João, who walked out of the kitchen with two cafezinhos and some toast. He motioned for me to sit down and he took the chair opposite me. He slid one of the two cups of liquid speed across the table to me. He let me take a sip before he spoke.

"Did Anjo take you to see the body?"

I nodded.

"Was it Nelson, like they're saying?"

I guessed he figured I'd know who Nelson was, since the guy had paid me a shitload of reais recently.

"Yeah, it was Nelson."

The name hung in the air for a second.

"It was Nelson and whoever took him out made him suffer."

"Like the others?"

"Exactly like the others, whip-marks and all."

João shook his head.

"Did you know him, João? Did you know Nelson?"

"Yeah, I knew him, but just from being the local cambista, you know, the guy running the local bicho operation."

"Any idea of where he lived?"

He shook his head.

"Nah, but Anjo would know that."

I stuffed some toast in my mouth. It was crunchy and way past over-buttered. Another reason to move to Brazil.

"I'd like to check his apartment, but the cops have probably got it sealed off."

João burst into laughter. I didn't quite get the joke.

"You're talking like you're still in New York, where the cops will actually investigate a murder. The only reason any cop might have gone by Nelson's place is to rob it because they know he's dead. They don't seal anything off here in Brazil. If you find his place, you can look around all you want. Guaranteed. Oh, and by the way, he probably doesn't have an apartment."

"What's he got then? A house?"

João shook his head.

"He's probably got a room somewhere. A room with a mattress and a couple of chairs. And the chairs will be gone if the cops have been there already."

It looked like Anjo and I had a program for the evening. João and I finished our toast in silence, then went our separate ways. My way was to wander over to the Lacerda Elevator and down to the Sweet St. Pete. I was looking for a semblance of normality, a term I'd never really associated with my cousin. Any port in a storm, I guess.

I found Bones seated on the dock chatting with the dockside skinnies. They opened the circle when they saw me coming and someone handed me a beer. Everyone murmured something about Nelson being a hell of a guy, a "porreta" in Portuguese, then they drifted away, leaving me and Bones in an awkward silence. Bones motioned toward the boat.

"Let's get out of the sun, Cuz."

It was good to step into the shade and even better to sit my ass down. Bones rubbed his face and looked at me. I looked back.

"So you gonna tell me? Or you gonna make me guess?"

I ran the whole story by him, from João's wake-up knock to Anjo driving away in his taxi, with all of the gory details. He didn't say much, but his eyes reacted at all the right points in the story. I think he exhaled harder than me when I finished.

"Whoa, dude! You've had a hell of a day and it's only one-thirty."

"I'd like for it to be over already."

"So what're you going to do?"

I wanted to say something confident, something full of bravado, but I knew Bones too long to think he'd buy it. The truth was that beyond maybe checking Nelson's apartment, if he had one and if Anjo knew where it was, I had no other plans. So that's what I said. Bones nodded.

"Well, you've got to start somewhere."

"What about you, Bones?"

"What about me?"

"Well, how much longer are you planning to stick around here? Don't you have a family to get back to?"

"Last time I checked I did. I'm thinking about heading north sometime next week. You want a ride?"

"No, the ocean still scares me."

"Me, too, but I can't just leave this big boat here."

"Who's going to crew with you?"

"Not sure yet, but there'll be some interest."

"How's that work?"

"Ah, I get them to Miami and they catch another boat back or they come back by plane."

"How hard is that to do?"

He shrugged.

"Seems to happen all the time, so it can't be too hard. I'll figure it out. What're you gonna do until Anjo shows up?"

It was my turn to shrug.

"I think I'll take a walk, a nap and maybe another walk."

"Is there going to be a funeral?"

"Good question. Maybe I'll be able to answer it when Anjo shows up."

"Well, you can stick around here if you feel like watching me try to get this baby sea-worthy."

"I'll pass. The walk sounds more interesting. Better scenery involved."

"All right, man. Let me know if I can help."

"I will, Bones."

I drained my beer and stepped off the dock. Normalcy was still out of reach, but it was about as close as it could be under the circumstances.

CHAPTER 34

I WANDERED BACK TO the Lacerda Elevator and rode to the upper city. I hung a left on Misericordia Street and kept walking, trying to wear myself out so I could sleep a little. I drifted down the street, passing people of every conceivable shade of white, tan, brown or black as I went. Suddenly, my personal fog lifted and I found myself in the Largo do Pelourinho. An image of Nelson being whipped forced its way into my brain and I wished I could retreat back into my fog. Then somebody tapped me on the shoulder.

"Boa tarde, Mike Breza. Tudo bem?"

I was about as far from "everything okay?" as I'd ever been in my life, but I turned around anyway. It turned out to be a good move because I found myself face to face with Wanda Miranda.

"Wanda Miranda, como vai?"

She smiled at me and motioned for me to follow her. She led me to a small cafeteria on Tabuão Street, just around the corner. The kid working the tables bowed his head when she stepped over to the table in the shade and immediately brought her two Cokes, one of which she passed to me. She clinked her bottle against mine and took a sip. I did the same and it really hit the spot. Nothing like cold caffeine and sugar water on a hot afternoon. Then she looked over at me and spoke some English.

"Your day is not good?"

I had to smile. She was the first Brazilian I'd met with the gift of understatement.

"You could say that. But I think a better word for my day so far is 'merda'."

She chirped a bird-like laugh.

"Yes, I think merda is a good word."

"Did you know Nelson?"

She nodded.

"Um bom cambista e um homem melhor."

I already knew that he was a good cambista as well as a nice guy, but it was helpful to hear Wanda Miranda confirm my good impressions.

"Yeah, he was. Foi isso e mais."

She looked intently at me for a couple of seconds.

"What you do now?"

I didn't know and that's what I told her. She sipped her Coke and I did the same. When she finished, she stood up.

"Voce precisa vir comigo."

If Wanda Miranda thought I needed to go with her, that was good enough for me. She left some money on the table for the drinks, making it clear that bad things would happen to me if I tried to pay, and we walked back over to the Largo do Pelourinho. There she pulled aside a taxi driver, who, by the looks of the conversation, was only too glad to be in a position to help the one and only Wanda Miranda. We both climbed in the taxi and the guy shot out of his parking space like his day's wages depended on it. He did a one-eighty, floored it down Carmo Street, took a left, dealt with both vehicular and pedestrian traffic and squealed to the right. When I worked up the courage to look through my fingers, I saw that we were on France Avenue heading north. At this point it seemed safe to ask a couple of questions.

"Okay, Wanda, where are we going? Para onde vamos?"

The taxi driver shot me a look of surprise via the rearview mirror, then shifted his glance over to Wanda, who just smiled. She then turned to look at me.

"We go to see the father, Oxala. We go to Church of Bonfim."

She could see that I would've spent the rest of the trip trying to figure out what that meant, so she gave me some background. Oxala was the most respected of the orixas, the saints associated with the Afro-Brazilian religion of Candomble, and was considered the father of the others. In the days back when the Pelourinho was the center of civil entertainment instead of tourism, the African slaves had adopted the names of certain Catholic saints to cover their own religious customs. In the process, Oxala had become associated with O Senhor do Bonfim, which translated roughly as the Lord of the Good End or Lord of the Good Finish. Legend was that whoever bought a ribbon from the people selling in front of the Bonfim Church and tied three knots in the ribbon in securing it to his or her wrist, would be granted three wishes. The catch was that the wishes wouldn't be granted until the ribbon broke due to natural causes. I didn't ask what qualified as a natural cause, I just assumed pulling it off in a fit of rage or frustration wouldn't get me my wishes.

It took us about half an hour to get to the church, which, judging from the map in the back of the taxi, was on the less phallic end of a small peninsula that jutted out into the Bay of All Saints. We passed the Boa Viagem beach, where I had visited the widow of the second of the increasing number of murder victims. The church had its own plaza, not far from the water like everything else in Salvador, at the top of a very slight elevation. It was a blinding white in the afternoon sun, with a huge bell tower on either side of the entrance and an impressive cross in between the towers. The roof looked like it was made of red tile and the whole building was surrounded by an iron fence, not much different from the one I had peered through just hours before. The main entrance was huge and the door that blocked it had to weigh more than a three-story brick building. All in all, it was a magnificent church. Oxala, the daddy of all the orixas, had himself one fine crib.

We got out of the taxi in front of the church and the taxi driver refused to take our money, confirming once again the local esteem for Wanda Miranda. It occurred to me that I could use someone like her in New York City to keep the cost of my public transportation down. The area wasn't deserted, but it wasn't exactly a beehive of activity, either. For one thing, there was no real shade to be found and the sun was merciless to the point that the only three vendors in sight were huddled together on the shady side of the church in a desperate attempt to keep their plastic merchandise from melting. The sun didn't seem to faze Wanda one bit. She knelt in front of the building with her head bowed for several minutes. I thought I was going to have to look for a medic, but she rose and headed for the shade, motioning for me to go with her. She didn't have to tell me twice. I felt like my hair was melting.

Once in the shade, I got a better look at the souvenir merchandise being offered. The few things that wouldn't have melted in the searing afternoon heat would probably have undergone some kind of spontaneous combustion if they had mistakenly wandered into the sun. I made a mental note to look up the Portuguese translation for "Buyer, beware" back at the hotel. Wanda was chatting up one of the vendors, a large, black woman dressed in the same layers of ornate white lace that Wanda usually wore to her restaurant gig. Wanda was doing most of the talking, with the other woman nodding her head in rhythm with Wanda's speech. When Wanda stopped for breath, the other woman reached over onto her tray of tchotchkes and handed something to Wanda. When Wanda produced a couple of reais, the woman just looked at the money, making no movement to take it. Wanda insisted and finally the woman took the money, but not without making it clear that she didn't want to do it. Wanda smiled and thanked her before walking over to me.

"Me extende o braço, seu Mike Breza."

I was still of a mind to do whatever Wanda Miranda told me short of walking into traffic, so I extended my arm as she had requested. She took a green ribbon that said "Souvenir of Bonfim" and tied it loosely around my right wrist, making sure to tie three small knots, one on top of the other, to keep it in place. She then handed me a small, brown, plastic knick-knack which looked like a hand in the shape of a fist, only with the thumb placed between the index and middle fingers such that the tip of the thumb peeked out slightly from between the fingers. I looked at it in my hand, then looked at her, hoping for an explanation, which wasn't long in coming.

It turned out that the fist with the thumb sticking through the index and middle fingers was known as a figa and was particularly adept at keeping the evil eye and innumerable other catastrophes at a safe distance from the wearer. I wasn't clear on whether it had to be given as a present to be effective or if its power was somehow enhanced if received as a gift. Either way, I was covered since I never would have thought about buying it on my own. Wanda also gave me a small chain so I could wear the figa around my neck in style. I looked at my wrist and touched the plastic decoration suspended from my neck. I wasn't sure I felt all that protected, but I was all for doing whatever I could to turn my luck around. I hadn't really thought about my three wishes, but at least two of them would have involved Teresa Cardoso. It was probably better not to mention that, so I limited myself to thanking Wanda Miranda for the help. I also asked if she wanted to ride back to the center of town with me, but she shook her head.

"Eu fico aqui um tempinho. Obrigada."

If she wanted to stay, I wasn't going to convince her otherwise. I thanked her again for her help and flagged a cab whose driver looked like he needed some fast moving air in his face. As I was about to get in, Wanda called over to me.

"Seu Mike, you think about wishes, yes?"

I looked back at her and told her I would.

On the ride back to the Hotel do Chile, I tried to not focus exclusively on my own physical pleasure for the three wishes and I decided my number one priority was to get some kind of break in the case. I marked that firmly in my mind as wish number one, then decided that I really didn't need two more wishes. I combined them both into a fantasy of more time with Teresa Cardoso, then made the official mental distinction that it was of a lower priority than wish number one. This thought process assuaged my conscience as my taxi driver fought the afternoon traffic.

CHAPTER 35

IT WAS ABOUT FOUR-THIRTY when I stepped into the lobby of the Hotel do Chile. João was talking on the phone behind the front desk and gave me a thumbs up. I figured out that I was hungry and decided to find some late lunch. I was about to step back out the door when João hung up and tapped me on the shoulder.

"Oy, Mike, there's some kid here to see you. He's over in the waiting area."

I walked over to the sofa with absolutely no idea of who this kid could be, but it didn't take me long to figure it out. He was still about five-seven with smooth, dark skin and a minimalist afro. He looked different without his mom's hand yanking his hair out by the roots, but he still had her face. When he saw me coming over, he stood up and looked at his flip-flops, trying to figure out what to do with his hands. I cut him a break by extending mine.

"Josue, como vai? Tudo bem?"

My standard greeting in Portuguese relaxed him to the point where he could lift his head to look at me and murmur in an almost audible way that everything was good. He immediately went back to studying the pattern in the worn rug we were standing on while making an "uhhh" sound that led me to think he might use some more real words any second. He opted instead for thrusting a handful of crumpled banknotes at me and making noises that sounded more like chewing than any language I'd ever heard. I gathered that he was paying me back the twenty-five reais he and his buddies had clipped when we'd first met on his home turf. He even lifted his eyes for a second and said he was sorry, a monumental task for a thirteen year old kid. I didn't know what to do, so I took the money ball and shoved it in my pocket. I was still hungry, so I asked him if he wanted something to eat. He shook his head, but changed his mind when I told him there was good pizza two blocks away.

I lied to him because the pizza wasn't all that good, but he didn't seem to notice. He wolfed down four slices to my one and a half and he drained two Cokes in between. He even got kind of chatty after the second slice and wound up telling me bits and pieces of the story of his life. I managed to stitch together that there was a father somewhere, but he wasn't sure who it was and his mom wasn't about to tell him. He'd finished the sixth grade and about a week of the seventh, but wasn't quite making it through the school door these days and he just wanted to find a real job to stay out of the drug trade. He'd seen a couple of kids younger than him wind up on the business end of a Glock and it had scared him. It occurred to me that it was a rare thirteen year old boy that could admit his fears. I couldn't have done it at his age, especially not with some guy I barely knew. Josue was an exceptional kid.

He asked me a little about being a private detective and my brief but detailed description of low pay, long hours and mind-numbing tedium disabused him of any notion about the profession's glamour. He wanted to know how I knew Anjo and I told him a Cliff Notes version of our adventure in New York. This impressed him somewhat, but then he asked me the real question he'd been wanting to spring since his first mouthful of pizza. He asked me whether I liked his mom. I gave him my best adult look in the eye and told him that I liked his mom a lot. Then I pulled out the ball of reais that he had given me at the hotel and rolled it across the table to him. I told him that I liked his mom too much to accept money from her son and that if he couldn't find anything better to do with it than give it to me, then he should buy his mom something that would make her happy. I explained that I appreciated the gesture, but that I wouldn't accept the money. Besides, the lesson I learned about wandering around an unfamiliar favela alone was worth at least twenty-five reais. He liked that explanation. I paid the bill and we stepped back out onto Chile Street.

It was about ten of six. I needed to get back to the hotel to wait for Anjo, so I shook hands with Josue and we split up. We both looked back over our shoulders and gave each other the classic Brazilian thumbs up. He was a good kid. I hoped he thought the same of me.

CHAPTER 36

ANJO WAS ALREADY AT the hotel when I stepped inside. He looked a whole lot better than when I had seen him that morning. His eyes were open and they were no longer red, so that was a good start. He also broke into a wide smile when he saw me and we threw our arms around each other, just like we'd ended the morning.

"You okay, Anj?"

"Tudo bem, Mike. Except for the obvious."

"Yeah, no more winning jogo do bicho tickets."

He cringed a little when I said it, but his grin told me that the black humor was just what was needed.

"So where to, Mr. Taxi Driver?"

"We start walking, my friend."

We stepped out on to Chile Street and cut over to Saldanha Da Gama Street, which ran us right into the Praça da Se. The buildings around us were ancient by New York standards, which meant they probably dated from the colonial period. Right on the plaza, all the facades had been restored, but a little beyond the extent of the typically superficial tourist view, the architecture was more of the crumbling variety. The constant bus traffic added to the charm, giving the buildings that delicate shade of gray that comes from years of leaded gasoline fumes spewing every which way. Anjo led me on to Laranjeiras Street and then on to a smaller street named Santa Isabel. There was a small alley up ahead on the right hand side whose most important function was to serve as a no-car-traffic soccer field for the local future Peles. It also separated two building entrances, one on either side of the alley about twenty feet in from where we stood.

Anjo wanted to take me in the entrance on the right hand side, but we had to wait for a break in the soccer game to step by. The inside of the building was damp and felt like fresh air only circulated through every other Christmas or so. The hallway was almost lit by a single struggling lightbulb hanging down from the ceiling with exposed wiring that was the single biggest fire hazard I'd ever seen. It was a New York Post headline waiting to happen and the only possible explanation for it not bursting into flames was that the laws of physics that the rest of the world lived by simply didn't apply in Salvador.

We climbed a narrow staircase to the fifth floor, where we pushed open a flimsy door that led onto a hallway that was even damper than the stairway. It was also even more poorly lit, if that was possible. We walked past several doorways, inside of which some very active family life was taking place, and stopped in front of a door with a metallic number fifty-five mounted on it.

It didn't look like it had been declared a crime scene, so Anjo opened the door. I didn't ask where he had gotten the key.

There was a window on the western wall of the narrow room we stepped into, so it was pretty well lit by the sun. Not that it mattered all that much, because there really wasn't much to see. There were two cots set up on the right of the door with a small chest of drawers next to them against the wall. A small table accompanied by two chairs was on the left and a television was parked on a wooden crate behind the table. There was a small refrigerator next to the TV and with that, the inventory was complete. I looked over at Anjo.

"Have you been here before, Anj?"

He nodded

"Does it look any different to you? Like someone has searched the place?"

Anjo shook his head.

"No, it looks like it always has."

It was one of the barest rooms I had ever been in. I looked around again. There were still no shelves, no cabinets and no visible sink. That meant I had another question to ask.

"So, Anj, where's the bathroom?"

He jerked his thumb toward the door.

"Down the hall. It's for everybody that lives on this floor."

That helped explain the dampness. Anjo spun around, examining the walls and mumbling something in Portuguese.

"What are you saying there, Anj?"

He did another one hundred eighty degrees and looked at me.

"I was saying to myself that it looks the same as always. No real furniture, no food and no Nelson. He spent so little time here, I don't know why he rented the room."

"Maybe he just wanted to have a place to call home. Like everybody else."

"Perhaps."

I did my own spin move and even ran my hands along the walls to see if there might be some kind of hiding place that was chock full of helpful evidence that would enable us to track down Nelson's killer. But since it was a real-life investigation and not a Hollywood movie set, we wound up leaving the room empty-handed. We both knew it was a long shot at best that we were going to find anything, but now that we were out of ideas, there wasn't much else to hang our hopes on.

It looked like halftime in the soccer game when we stepped out of the building, so we were able to step onto the field of play without causing too much interference. As we walked away, one of the kids at our backs made a sound like a police siren. Anjo kept walking like he hadn't heard it, but the small piece of my brain that wasn't thinking constantly about Teresa forced me to stop in my tracks. I grabbed Anjo's shoulder.

"Anjo, hey, Anjo."

"What is it, Mike?"

I looked back at the kid making the siren sound.

"Ask that kid why he's making that noise."

Anjo looked at me like I had just asked him to punch me in the face.

"Mike, he is making the noise because he is a young boy. That is why."

"No, man, ask him why he's making the noise and if the police have been here recently. If they have been, ask him who they came to see and if he knows why."

Anjo's eyes showed interest and he backtracked to where the boy was standing, next to his buddies and in front of the makeshift goal in the alleyway. I hung back until Anjo waved me forward.

"Mike, this is Edson."

I stuck out my hand and said "Moo-eetoo prahzer." Edson was not very impressed by my pronunciation, but he shook my hand anyway. I looked at Anjo.

"So what did he say?"

"He says that the police came about a week ago looking for Nelson, but that he wasn't here. He also says that Nelson came by later that same day and hasn't been here since."

"Nelson hasn't been here in a week and the cops haven't either? Is he sure? Nobody came today? Nobody's been here since Nelson died?"

I didn't wait for Anjo to translate and tried to ask Edson myself. I must've done a decent job of asking because I got the same answer as Anjo. The cops had been around a week ago looking for Nelson, hadn't found him and that was it. I also got the added bonus of being told I could ask around if I didn't believe him. I told him as best I could that I believed him and thanked him for the information. Then Anjo and I stepped off the soccer pavement because the second half was about to start. We had started walking back toward the Hotel do Chile when I decided I needed to think.

"Anj, I need to sit with a beer in front of me. Where can we go?"

His smile was more sad and tired than anything else, but it still managed to cut the falling darkness a little bit. I don't know where the hell he took me, but it was definitely a bar, complete with stools and a TV with little to no reception unless a soccer game was on. That seemed to be the standard for bar TV's in Brazil. Anjo asked for a couple of beers and we were set. Set for what I didn't know, but it was a start.

CHAPTER 37

SINCE THERE WAS NO soccer game on, I stared at the fuzzy TV screen while sipping my beer. Anjo did the same. There were bar noises around us; people talking, some laughter and glasses sliding across wooden surfaces. It reminded me of a slow night at the White Horse Tavern back in New York, which meant that my brain could start working.

"Okay, Anjo, so why would the cops go looking for Nelson at his apartment?"

I realized I was taking liberties by using the word apartment since Nelson's place made a shoebox look spacious. Anjo tipped his head to one side.

"There is only one possible reason."

He rubbed his thumb against his middle and ring fingers, making the universal sign for moolah. It looked like our two mediocre minds were thinking alike.

"You mean from the jogo do bicho, right?"

He nodded as I took a sip of my beer.

"So they were trying to shake him down?"

He gave me a puzzled look.

"I do not know what means shake him down."

"It means they wanted to get money from him on the sly."

Same puzzled expression.

"On the sly means without anybody else knowing."

This time his nod meant he understood. Money. They wanted money from Nelson.

"Anj, I know you told me about this before, but wouldn't a cambista like Nelson, a guy working at street level, have some kind of protection from the guys who really run the jogo? I mean, guys like Nelson are where the money is collected. Don't the jogo's owners watch out for their guys? You know, keep them from being hassled?"

Anjo thought about that for a second before answering me.

"The problem is that a cambista must be able to run his own territory. He can offer lower pricing, like Nelson did the first time you played. He can allow people to make bets on credit if he wants to. If the person doesn't pay, then the cambista must get the money somehow. He cannot ask for help from his bosses every time a problem appears. If the cambista cannot solve the problems in his own territory, the owners of the jogo will get someone else to do it. And there are a lot of people who would like the job of cambista. Nelson got it because he was smarter, faster and harder than the others. But all his bosses wanted from him was the money. They are not interested in the problems of the cambista. They are concerned only with the money they must pay out to keep the jogo in business and the money they collect for themselves."

It seemed like it was no different from being a bookie in New York City. When it came to collections, the only rule was "no excuses accepted." But to make the collection, the street level bookie was on his own. I was glad to see that at least one law of physics held true, even in Salvador. Shit still ran downhill. Nelson had to handle his own problems and dealing with the cops was a big task on his daily to-do list. But something else was still bugging me.

"So say the cops come looking for Nelson to supplement their public servant salaries. He tells them no deal. This pisses the cops off, but they still want some money. Why would they kill him? He's no good to them dead, right? Even if they don't get busted for killing a cambista, they've messed up a system that already involves a level of police with more firepower than them. Somebody's gonna get upset and these cops who did the murder are gonna get spanked."

Anjo looked at me with yet another puzzled expression.

"I do not understand your point, Mike."

"It's just that the cops shaking Nelson down would probably just slap him around a little. You know, to let him know they mean business. They wouldn't kill him. Dead men cut no checks."

Anjo thought for a second.

"Perhaps they only meant to beat him, but killed him by accident."

"Could be, but then why would they put his body on display at the church steps? Why the high volume advertising? Why not just ditch the body where nobody's going to find it for a long time? Any big city worth its urban troubles has got to have a ton of places to ditch a cadaver and who's going to know where better than a bunch of bad cops?"

I got a look that was less puzzled and more pensive. I also got a big dose of logic.

"They put Nelson's body on the steps to cover up their mistake of killing him. This way it is just another dead mulatto or black man and it looks like part of a crime pattern that already exists."

It was a good explanation, no doubt about it. Nelson had probably heard about the cops looking for him at his room and had decided not to go back. At work he was untouchable, seeing as how he provided an invaluable social service to all of Salvador, and if he was half the hustler Anjo described, he could probably stay off the police radar after work, figuring the heat would die down sooner or later. The problem was that even a city as big as Salvador started to feel real small after a few days on the run. And even the worst cops could get answers to their questions. Nelson had probably just run out of space and once the cops picked him up, they made their point too hard. I stared at my empty glass and I imagined Anjo was doing the same thing to his heart.

We left the bar and Anjo guided me back to the main stem. The beer had sapped my energy and I was ready for bed. When we got to the hotel, João had a note for me from Teresa. She'd passed by, but couldn't wait and said she'd try to catch up with me tomorrow. By then I'd probably be ready for some catching. I turned around to say good night to Anjo, but he had a question.

"Will you come to the funeral tomorrow, Mike?"

I hadn't even thought about it, but how could I refuse?

"Sure, Anjo, where and when?"

"Tomorrow morning at eleven o'clock at the Igreja do Santissimo Sacramento."

"The funeral is at the same church where he was found? Where all of them were found?"

Anjo nodded.

"There will be a number of people there, so try to arrive on time."

The irony of a Brazilian telling a New Yorker to be on time wasn't lost on either of us. He grinned at me and we called it a night.

CHAPTER 38

ELEVEN O'CLOCK HADN'T SEEMED like such an ambitious goal when I bedded down, but I knew I was in trouble when I opened my eyes and saw ten to ten staring me in the face. I barely had time to shower and dress before leaving for the funeral. Seeing as how my sartorial choices were limited, I just tried to make sure whatever I put on was within a stain or two of being clean. On my way out of the hotel, I caught a glimpse of the morning paper on the reception counter. The headline screamed "AGAIN!" and there was a gruesome close-up photo of Nelson's body that undoubtedly did wonders for the paper's circulation even while it stopped mine cold. I leaned in close to see the details of the photo and found what I was looking for. The photographer had managed to highlight the swastika carved in the middle of Nelson's back.

Another beautiful day was waiting for me when I stepped out of the hotel. I made for the Praça da Se, then headed toward the Pelourinho and Passo Street. The gates to the stairway leading up to the church entrance from Carmo Hill were open and there were at least fifty people hanging out on the steps. The crowd got thicker as I got closer to the church's entrance, where Anjo himself was one of the main attractions. There must have been fifteen people vying for his attention. Fortunately for me, my New York gringo appearance stood out in that particular crowd and Anjo had no trouble spotting me. He politely escaped his personal swarm and came over to give me a bear hug, which I tried my best to return with my arms pinned to my side.

"Bom dia, Mike. You arrived on time."

I didn't bother telling him how I'd almost overslept.

"Looks like half of Salvador did the same. Are all these people friends of Nelson?"

Anjo shrugged.

"Friend, clients, neighbors. They have all come to express their sorrow."

I saw Edson, the kid who told us about the cops looking for Nelson, down on the stairs. He gave me the what's-up-nod and I returned the gesture. Anjo than grabbed me by the arm to walk me into the church. It was like stepping into a greenhouse gearing up for Mother's Day. Both sides of the main aisle were lined with more flower arrangements than Imelda Marcos had shoes. We hacked our way through the fragrant underbrush to the altar, where Nelson was laid out in a coffin that looked about twice the size of his apartment. The box itself was ornately carved wood with cushions so plush I felt like asking Nelson to slide over and let me take the load off my feet. His new crib was definitely a step up in terms of luxury. It seemed a little unusual. I would've expected a man of Nelson's means to be buried in a few cardboard boxes taped together. I tapped Anjo on the shoulder.

"Anjo, where did the money for all the flowers and the coffin come from?"

"It came from the owners of the jogo do bicho."

"You mean to tell me they forked over the cash to pay for all this?"

He nodded.

"All this and the Mass, too."

"The Mass?"

"It's not free, my friend."

"These guys must have thought pretty highly of Nelson."

"He was a good cambista who made a lot of money for them. They always take care of things that are important to the families of the workers. Even those with no family like Nelson."

I looked around at the growing crowd.

"Well, he might not have any family to speak of, but he sure had a ton of friends."

"Muito certo."

I felt a hand on my shoulder and turned around to see Bones. He seemed out of breath.

"Hey, Cuz. I came running as soon as I heard about the funeral. Anj, how's it going? I'm real sorry about Nelson. He seemed like a hell of a guy."

Bones gave Anjo the hug-and-two-back-slaps consolation combo, then stepped back next to me.

"I apologize for showing up in shorts, but the dock boys just told me about the funeral fifteen minutes ago. It was all I could do to get here on time without stopping to change."

I looked at him.

"Change into what? A less dirty pair of shorts?"

"Pretty much, yeah."

Anjo smiled.

"It is more than enough that you are here. Nelson was not a formal man."

I felt another hand on my shoulder and this time the turnaround was even better. It was Teresa Cardoso, wearing a white dress made from the same kind of lacey material that Wanda Miranda was wearing the first time we saw her at the restaurant down by the docks. It looked better on Teresa, so much so that I was speechless. She kissed me on the lips, then stepped over to give her condolences to Anjo. Bones gave me a well-placed elbow to the ribs.

"What the hell have you been doing in your spare time and why haven't you invited me?"

"Well, for starters, you have a wife and kid."

"Okay, I admit that's a slight impediment, but you could've at least prepared me for the envy in my future."

"I'm having a hard time understanding how a man who is retired in his forties with no foreseeable financial worries and who is tooling around South America on his sailboat for grins is going to be envious of me. Did I already mention the beautiful wife and daughter?"

"Uh, yes, you did."

"Good, I would hate to leave them out. So what's this envy thing again?"

"Okay, point made and taken, but the least you could do is introduce me."

I made the introduction when Teresa came back over and after a second look at that white dress, I decided that maybe Bones was right. Right then he had every reason to be envious of me. I asked her if she knew Nelson very well and she nodded as if to say "a little bit". Bones couldn't resist.

"Don't be an idiot, Mike. She came to be with you. Ela veio para estar com voce."

I asked her if it was true.

"Isso e certo, Teresa?"

She put her hand behind my head, pulling down ever so slightly to kiss me before she responded.

"Claro, meu bem."

CHAPTER 39

I REMEMBER THAT PEOPLE started taking seats because the Mass was about to start. I remember that Anjo came over and slid into the pew first, followed by Bones and Teresa and I remember that I had the aisle seat. But I don't remember much about the Mass because I spent the whole time next to Teresa with her knee touching mine. The celestial trimmings of Nelson's send-off made a nice contrast with the deeply profane thoughts running through my mind. I hadn't known Nelson well enough to predict his final destination, but I was pretty sure that his paradise was nothing compared to the heaven on earth that I was headed for after Mass. I tried to feel guilty about it, but my Catholic school training was no match for temptation. Thank God.

Everyone lined up at the end of Mass to pay our final respects. With Teresa's hand on my arm, I thought my heart was going to pump its way out of my chest. We were in line silently for awhile when I suddenly realized

I had my last winning ticket from the jogo do bicho in my pocket. Anjo was in front of us, so I tapped his shoulder and asked if I could leave it in the casket with Nelson. He gave me a thumbs up and smiled, so I tucked it in between Nelson's arm and the box's expensive lining. Maybe it would bring him as much luck as it had brought me. We then followed the line of people out of the church.

The sun was still shining high in the sky when we stepped out, having refused to alter its daily course in spite of Nelson's passing. I was about to ask Anjo about the burial when something at the bottom of the steps leading up to the church caught my eye. It was a couple of things, actually, one of which was a black sedan and the other a cop. But it wasn't just any cop; it was my friend Delegado Neto. It looked like his playmates were inside the car, behind the tinted glass. I got the impression that he was waiting for someone, an impression that was confirmed when he waved me over. I had to convince Teresa to not walk over with me. Anjo and Bones were told to stay put by the delegado himself.

Things started pleasantly enough.

"Boa tarde, Senhor Breza."

"Boa tarde, Delegado Neto."

He was smiling, but it was a smile that would've given Frosty the Snowman the shivers.

"I see you have come to your friend Nelson's funeral."

"With a hundred other people, yeah."

"How well did you know Nelson?"

"Not as well as everybody else here. I've only been in Brazil for a couple of days."

That was when the conversation took a turn for the worse. He dropped the cigarette he'd been smoking and put it out with a twist of his foot. His smile went from cold to arctic.

"Senhor Breza, would you mind coming with us down to the delegacia?"

"Is the delegacia police headquarters?"

"Yes, it is. Please excuse my poor English."

The quality of his English wasn't what worried me at that moment. I was more concerned with what he was planning to do to me down at HQ. Unfortunately, my options for responding were limited.

"I'd be happy to do so. May I ask why?"

"I think we have some things to talk about."

"Can I inform my partner about where I'm going?"

He extended his arm as if to invite me to do so.

"Please do, Senhor Breza."

I had to work real hard against the instinct to flee as I walked the five steps back over to Anjo, Teresa and Bones, whose first question hit me after only four steps.

"Mikey, what does he want?"

"He wants me to go down to headquarters with them."

"On what charge?"

"I don't think I'm under arrest. He says he just wants to talk."

Anjo spoke up.

"We will go down to the delegacia to wait for you."

Teresa wanted to know what was going on.

"Podem me dar uma ideia sobre o problema aqui? Porra, eu não falo ingles."

When Anjo and Bones informed her simultaneously, she wasn't crazy about the idea. She grabbed my arm and begged me not to go. She was dry-eyed, but there were tears in her voice for sure. Anjo whispered in her ear not to make a scene in front of the cops, but I was sure even the guys in the car had looked up from their dirty magazines to see what the fuss was about. For better or worse, they had made Teresa as the gringo's girlfriend. I hoped it wasn't something I would regret later.

Delegado Neto opened the rear passenger door for me, but was polite enough not to cuff me or push my head down as I slid into the back seat. The guy next to me was one of the two I had seen watching Nelson's place of business back when it seemed like winning the jogo do bicho was a great thing. He was wearing a nice pair of Ray-Bans and looked like a rumpled refugee from Men In Black. I'd never seen the driver before, but his shades were also pretty nice and his suit just as dark. That made Delegado Neto Tommy Lee Jones, only a lot more deadpan. His smile was colder, too. As the car pulled away from the curb, I caught a glimpse of Teresa crying in her hands. That scared me more than Delegado Neto's smile.

CHAPTER 40

NOBODY SEEMED TO FEEL like chatting, so I just kept my mouth shut, too. I tried to figure out what streets we were on for the first two minutes, but gave up when I remembered that I only really knew where Chile Street was. After a number of twists and turns, we somehow wound up at the same stationhouse on Alfredo de Brito Street where I had initiated my friendship with Delegado Neto. I could feel my nostalgia starting to rise when we passed the same cop seated at the entrance desk as my previous visit. He didn't roll his eyes at me like before. This time he gave me more of an icy grin and I wondered if he'd practiced it with Delegado Neto earlier that day. My friends led me to a small, windowless room with a rectangular table that wasn't crippled and three chairs that were. They led me in, indicated that I should sit in the worst of the three chairs, then left the room. I decided to keep my worrying from exploding into full-blown panic until they returned.

I must've sat there for thirty minutes, enough time to count the holes in the cinderblock walls and see how many different triangles I could make by connecting them at random in my mind. It was actually kind of peaceful, but Delegado Neto's grand entrance brought all that to a halt with the banging of the door against the wall. Even though I knew he was about my height, he seemed taller standing in the door frame. His moustache looked darker, too, but that could've been the poor lighting. I was somewhat encouraged to see that all he was carrying was a pad of paper and a pencil. I didn't think the pad would do much damage, unless he used it to pound the pencil through my cheek. That didn't seem too likely, but when I saw Detective Santos walk in behind Neto with his hands in his pockets, I wondered if he might be carrying a heavier utensil or something sharper than a pencil. Santos positioned himself in a corner behind Neto and leaned against the wall with his arms folded. Neto pulled out the chair across from me and sat down like he was in his living room. He looked a lot more relaxed than I did. He wrote the date and time on the top sheet of the pad, then looked at me with his best I'm-the-cop-here-and-you're-not stare.

"Mr. Breza, why were you at the funeral?"

The question seemed innocuous enough.

"I was paying my respects to Nelson."

"How well did you know Nelson?"

"I met him when I played the jogo do bicho, that's it."

"So why was it so important for you to be at the funeral?"

"Nelson was a good friend of some people I've met here in Salvador. I won the jogo from him. It just seemed like the respectful thing to do."

He tapped his pencil against the pad and started to doodle while he asked his next question.

"I also saw you at the church the morning Nelson's body was found. What were you doing there?"

"Well, as you probably recall from my first visit to the stationhouse, I'm a free-lance journalist and the story of the bodies on the church steps was somehing I had been pursuing. Somebody came to my hotel shortly after the body was discovered and let me know it was there. I got dressed and ran over."

"So you were in bed when the murder took place?"

"I don't know when the murder took place, but I was in bed from about 10:30 on."

"Did anyone see you go to bed?"

I nodded. He scratched out one doodle and started another, even when he looked up at me.

"Who can confirm that you were in bed?"

"A woman I was with."

"Her name?"

"Teresa."

"Is she a prostitute?"

"No, she isn't."

"Are you sure? There are many prostitutes in Salvador. Many of them are black."

He was trying to get me to lose my cool. This meant he thought I still had a cool to lose, which in turn made me doubt his police instincts. Any cool I'd possessed had gone AWOL the instant he'd invited me to ride in the black sedan. I'd managed to keep from visibly quaking, but you'd think an experienced delegado would smell the fear and not waste time trying to produce something that was already filling up the room. This meant that I had to be a little more obvious in giving him what he wanted. I leaned forward on the table for theatrical purposes.

"Look, Delegado Neto, I'm not sure why you brought me down here, but I want to assure you that I'm not trying to create any problems for you. You made it clear that the jogo do bicho is illegal, I promised you that I wouldn't go near it again and I haven't. I went to the funeral out of respect for Anjo, but I didn't really know Nelson and I went to see the body on the church steps without knowing it was him. I really don't want any trouble. I'm a visitor in this country and I just want to enjoy my stay here without any problems. I know I was rude to you the first time we met and I apologize for that. I lost my temper and I shouldn't have done it. It won't happen again. I swear to you that you won't have any problems with me."

As I spoke I put a little crack in my voice. The faintest hint of a smile tugged at both ends of Delegado Neto's lips and I knew that he had gotten what he was looking for. Still, the rules demanded that he give me a little kick while I was down. He gave me a good, stern cop face and laid down the law.

"And no more prostitutes either. That is also illegal here in Brazil. You stay away from this…"

He leaned over to consult his doodles.

"…Teresa."

He was waiting to see if I objected to his calling her a prostitute. Any protest on my part would mean he hadn't broken me the way he wanted. But it was still his house, so I gave him a very sincere head nod and looked down at the table. While I waited the extra beat with my eyes down to underscore my place in the social pecking order, I happened to glance at his doodles. Most of them were pretty well scratched out, but the last one was still plainly visible. The man had spent his time between questions sketching swastikas.

CHAPTER 41

DELEGADO NETO AND DETECTIVE Santos filed out of the interrogation suite, leaving me cooling my heels for anther twenty minutes before a uniform came and led me back out to the exit. Anjo, Bones and Teresa were all waiting and practically threw themselves at me when the uniform cut me loose.

"Hey, guys, I've only been locked up for like an hour and a half."

That was all the talking I could do with Anjo squeezing the air out of my lungs and Teresa pumping more in as she kissed me. Bones limited himself to slapping me on the back. It was nice to be popular again, if only for a moment.

We stepped outside into the mid-afternoon sun and with my fear pretty much fully subsided, I realized that I was hungry. It was a consensus feeling so Anjo led us back toward the Praça da Se and into another hole in the wall restaurant with furniture that dated from the mid-nineteen fifties. Rice and beans never tasted so good. It must have been the extra helping of freedom.

Once the three of them figured out that I was no worse for the wear, they all wanted to know what had gone on. I gave them a pretty good blow-by-blow description, leaving out Delegado Neto's attempts to paint Teresa as a prostitute. By the time we'd finished our rice and beans, it was four o'clock and we were all sipping cafezinhos. Anjo was impressed by the fact that I had gotten out of the police station with no visible bruises, Bones was impressed that I didn't come out in a box and I was highly impressed with the sight of Teresa's legs as they stretched out under the table. I could've started to feel inadequate, but the adrenaline tsunami in my veins was having none of that. Bones broke my concentration with a question.

"So the point of taking you to the stationhouse was just to scare you?"

I shook my head.

"Nah, Bones, it was to scare me even more than I already was."

Anjo finished his cafezinho before chiming in.

"Do you think that was the only reason?"

"It had to be, Anj. There was nothing else to be gained from talking to me. He has to know more about the murders than I do."

Anjo scratched the back of his head.

"If he does, he is doing his best to ignore it, just like the rest of the police."

I was looking Anjo in the eye, but all I could concentrate on was Teresa's fingers resting on my knee under the table. Anjo kept talking, but I really didn't hear him anymore. The tsunami was roaring in my ears.

We finished eating and left the restaurant. I had only one thing on my mind and it looked like Teresa was on my wavelength as well. Both Bones and Anjo were subtle enough to discreetly melt away, but not before Anjo said he'd look me up later that night after I'd had a chance to rest. His excuse for leaving was that he had to go play taxi driver, but he wasn't going to get much of a tip from his first customer. Bones waved at me from the passenger side as they pulled away.

I remember asking Teresa if she wanted to walk with me and I have a hazy memory of drifting down Misercordia Street toward the Lacerda Elevator with her hand in mine. The last thing I remember about being on Chile Street with her is how beautiful her smile was. Then we were on our way up to my room. When we got to the door, I asked her if she was sure she wanted to come in with me. She knew that I knew the answer and she knew that I just wanted to hear her say the words again.

"Claro, meu bem."

I was born without the words I needed to describe the next couple of hours and I hadn't learned them in my thirty-four years of life, either. All I know is that the tsunami receded little by little, leaving me flat on my back with my legs intertwined with hers. Neither of us could move and we both drifted away for a little while. At some point, she kissed me on the cheek and said she was going to take a bath. She invited me in with her, but I couldn't move just yet. She said she'd wait for me in the tub and I started to drift off again. I wasn't asleep, but I could see the chat room I had been sitting in with Delegado Neto and Detective Santos. I saw myself talking with them and I saw his doodles again. It was a bigger, darker swastika than I remembered and Delegado Neto started asking me about the jogo do bicho. At that point, my eyes popped open, telling me rest time was over.

I could hear Teresa in the bathtub sighing with delight. It was music to my ears, so I stepped into the bathroom and helped her scrub her back, hoping to hear some more music. Then I got into the tub behind her, she leaned back on my chest and we soaked. I've never been one for extending my tub time beyond what was absolutely needed, but this was one bath that I had no problem stretching out.

We were a couple of prunes by the time we finished soaking. The hotel towels were like tissue paper, only less absorbent, but they felt pretty good as I rubbed them against her back. I dried myself with a hand towel and threw my own clothes on fast so I could watch her dress. It was almost as much fun as watching her undress. It was scary how much I liked watching her adjust her skirt. As we rode down in the elevator, I asked her if she knew a place where we could get something to eat. She looked at her feet, then raised her eyes to say that she couldn't stay because she had to go home and check on Josue. I told her that I understood and asked when I could see her again. She smiled and said as soon as she could do it. The answer made my heart and other body parts soar.

CHAPTER 42

I STOOD IN FRONT of the entrance, watching her walk away in the dusk. As she swayed into the distance, I felt a little guilty for enjoying myself so much when I was there to help a friend solve some murders. I managed to get over it as Teresa faded from view. Then I saw Anjo crossing the street from where he'd just parked his taxi. He gave me one of his typical high-voltage smiles and I gave him a very Brazilian thumbs-up gesture in return.

"Did you manage to rest, Mike?"

His shit-eating grin told me he already knew the answer.

"As much as I could under the circumstances. Thanks for giving me a break. Did you make any money?"

Anjo shook his head without losing the grin.

"No, I also rested like you did."

"Who's the lucky girl?"

"Maybe you will meet her before you return to New York."

"As long as her name isn't Ashley, you've got nothing to worry about from me."

Ashley Martin was a would-be girlfriend of mine that Anjo had managed to fall into bed with on his visit to New York.

"Ah, you still remember that? It was so long ago!"

"Seems like it, doesn't it? Let's go look for Bones and get something to eat. We need to think about our next move."

It was a beautiful fall night in Salvador by the time we reached the Sweet St. Pete, where Bones piped us aboard. He was slouched in one of his flimsy deck chairs with a beer in hand and offered us a pair of equally decrepit seats. He looked like he needed some rest himself.

"So both of you guys went off to get laid while I busted my ass here getting my rig ready for the long ride home. There's no justice, man. When do I get mine?"

"Bones, I believe we've already been through this once today. A man in your position ain't gonna get much sympathy from the likes of me and Anjo. At least you have something to go home to."

Anjo wanted in on the razzing action.

"Yes, Mike, but your cousin is certainly not returning home to a woman like Teresa Cardoso."

"No, Anj, I guess he's not. Nor is he returning home to any of your multiple girlfriends."

Bones grinned and feigned indignance.

"Multiple girlfriends? Did you say multiple? You see, Cuz? That's what I'm talking about. No justice at all, man."

Silence reigned for all of thirty seconds. In that time we could hear the creaking of the boats as they bobbed in the water. I could almost pretend that there weren't four bodies floating around in the back of my mind. Then Bones reeled them in to the here and now.

"So what do you make of Nelson's murder, Mikey?"

I really didn't know what to say, but I talked anyway.

"Well, it looks like the only difference between Nelson and the others is that I'd actually met the guy before he was killed. The MO is the same; torture by whip before death with a swastika chaser. It looks like the same sicko or group of sickos, but at this point, in New York everybody would be speculating about the possibility of a copycat killer."

Anjo was a little puzzled.

"What is this cat killer?"

I straightened him out.

"The term is copycat killer. In English, a copycat is someone who imitates somebody else. A copycat killer is someone twisted enough to imitate some serial killer's style in order to get some media attention for himself. If two different people are murdering their victims with the same method, the investigation gets a little complicated. Not that it isn't already."

Anjo was appropriately disgusted.

"What kind of person would do that?"

Bones had the answer.

"I don't really know, but with the U.S. having almost three hundred million people, you're bound to get some people whose ideas fall outside the societal norm. Sometimes way outside. Take these murders here in Salvador. It takes a real perverted individual to want to kill a man just because of the color of his skin."

His comment hung in the air just long enough for me to finally start thinking.

"Wait a minute, wait a minute, what if it's more than just the color of their skin?"

The look Anjo gave me was a mixture of curiosity and "huh?".

"What do you mean?"

"I mean, what if there's some other connection between these victims? Anjo, do you remember what you said last night? That the cops might've dumped Nelson's body on the church steps to cover up the mistake of killing him while trying to shake him down for some jogo do bicho money? What if this whole racist angle in the other murders is just a cover-up for something else? What if racism isn't the reason these guys died?"

I felt myself warming to the subject somewhat.

"What if we're chasing the wrong lead? We've looked for local racist groups and come up with a couple of punk rockers. We looked at an imported racist and came up with a born-again, hate-free pacifist with a swastika tattoo. Maybe it's not race-related at all. Maybe it's something else."

Both Bones and Anjo looked like they had their thinking caps on. I was trying to put on a pensive face myself, when my cousin's brainstorm hit.

"What about the jogo do bicho?"

He had to have more in mind, so I pushed him.

"What about it?"

"Look, the only thing we know about Nelson is that he was a cambista for the jogo do bicho, right? If he was killed for reasons related to the jogo, could that be the case with the other guys as well?"

Michael Featherstone

I was skeptical.

"Hold on, Bones. I asked if the victims had been involved in any illegal activities and everybody vouched for them. There's no way these guys were in the jogo, right Anjo?"

Anjo's pensive face was in full bloom. He closed his eyes and nodded his head ever so slightly.

"No, Mike, the three victims did not work in the jogo, but Flavio Guimarães had a cousin named Patricio that works for a cambista in the jogo."

"What does this cousin do for the cambista?"

Anjo shrugged.

"I do not know exactly. He may help with the money or the customers."

The connection with the jogo seemed interesting, but I wasn't really convinced.

"Okay, the fact that there's somebody in Flavio's family that works in the jogo makes it worth our while to talk with the guy, but how close was Flavio with his cousin? I have cousins I've never even met."

"And I've got cousins I wish I'd never met."

Bones never passed up a chance for a one-liner. It was one of the things I liked most about him. Anjo got the joke, but had more important things to say.

"Oh, they were cousins by blood, but they were more like brothers. They were the same age and their mothers were sisters who lived next door to each other and never had any other children. Flavio and Patricio were always with each other."

My doubts about the effect of Flavio's murder on his cousin were laid to rest. We needed to have a conversation with Patricio.

"Okay, we need to talk with this Patricio guy, Anj. Any idea of where we can find him?"

"I think he works near the Igreja do Bonfim."

"Bonfim? I was just out there yesterday."

Bones looked at me in disbelief.

"You were at the Bonfim Church? You? What the hell were you doing there?"

"I was told I had to go."

"By who, the cops?"

"Nah, a higher authority."

"Who's that?"

I looked at Anjo.

"Wanda Miranda, who else?"

Anjo laughed and Bones nodded his head.

"I got it. The pastry lady. She's a mãe de santo, too, right?"

"Yeah, but she seems more like the mayor of this town if you ask me. Look, Anjo, we have to talk with Jorge Arruda's wife, Sandra, about any friend or family member Jorge might have had working in the jogo and then we'll have to do the same with Teresa's sister, Maria. Can we do that?"

Anjo was more enthusiastic than I'd seen him since we'd learned about Nelson's death.

"We can start right now."

I looked over at Bones.

"You want in, Bones? It was your idea."

He looked around at his boat, although I couldn't figure out what he could possibly see in the dark.

"Sure, why not? This way I can observe more detective work first hand. You never know when I might need to change professions."

CHAPTER 43

WE SCRAMBLED OFF THE boat to Anjo's taxi in the upper city. The first stop was Gregorio de Matos Street, where Sandra Arruda lived. It was already eight-thirty when we knocked on the door, but she was glad to see us. She probably figured that our presence meant some progress was being made in the case. Anjo got right to the point, asking her if any of her husband's friends or relatives had been involved with the jogo do bicho in any way. She averted her eyes when Anjo asked the question and I knew we had something. It turned out that Jorge's half-brother, Armando, did some work for a cambista who did business in the Barra area of Salvador, near the lighthouse. She had no idea of where he lived, but knew that his corner was on Oceanic Avenue somewhere. It was a little late to go trolling for Armando out on the street, so I made a note of where we might find him and turned for the door. Just as we were about to step out, Sandra asked if we were getting any closer to solving the case. Anjo opened his mouth to speak, but I thought it would be better if the lie came from me. I told her in my best Portuguese that we had an idea that we were checking and that we would let her know as soon as we had some facts. She thanked me with a smile and Anjo and Bones followed me out the door. When we hit the street, Bones had the million dollar question.

"Do you think she realizes that there are no facts in Brazil?"

Even I knew the answer to that one.

"Better than you and me, pal."

Our next stop was the beach of Monte Serrat and the gravity-defying shack of Carlos de Souza's wife, Maria. I was particularly interested in this stop since Teresa might be in the vicinity. Given the sparse evening traffic, it only took us about fifteen minutes to get there. I spent most of the ride hypnotized, staring out at the moonlight as it danced on the bay. Even the grinding poverty that dominated the neighborhood we stepped into couldn't take away from the beauty of that sight.

We reached Maria's shack at around nine-thirty, but there was still plenty of activity all around. People had plastic chairs set up in front of their homes or were gathered in groups around radios or boom boxes that filled the air with everything from samba to Brazilian rap music. It was about seventy-five degrees on a clear, star-filled night and the outdoor lounges were open for business. Kids ran around playing tag or improvised soccer games while the adults relaxed. Life didn't look half bad at that moment in time.

Anjo refrained from knocking, just like he did the first time we visited, calling Maria's name instead. There was no answer from inside, but Josue appeared from around the back of the shack to see who was calling. He looked a little startled to see Anjo with a couple of white guys, but then he recognized me and smiled. He gave us all the soul handshake that was so common in Brazil, while Anjo asked for his aunt, saying we had some important questions to ask her. Josue replied that she was over at his mom's house and my ears perked right up. He then led us through a maze of shacks and footpaths that would have intimidated Lewis and Clark, finally stopping in front of his home sweet home. It was similar to Maria's place, built of sticks, stray boards and corrugated tin, all held together by a couple of prayers. It looked one stiff breeze shy of falling in on itself, but the décor, consisting of Teresa Cardoso seated in front, was one of the most attractive I'd ever seen. Maria was seated there, too, but she was background as far as my eyes were concerned.

Both ladies stood up when they saw us coming and Teresa's shocked look melted into a smile that made my heart pound faster. After the greetings, Anjo explained that we had come to ask a few more questions about her husband, Carlos. Anjo never got past the first question since it turned out that Carlos' best friend, Paulo Amado, whose name we had already heard according to my notes, worked for a cambista somewhere near the Pelourinho. He was nothing more than a gopher for the cambista, but his paycheck came from the jogo do bicho. That made it three for three on our bodies. Flavio Guimarães' cousin, Patricio, was running numbers up near the Bonfim Church, Jorge Arruda's half-brother, Armando clocked in for a cambista in the Barra area on Oceanic Avenue and now Paulo Amado, Carlos de Souza's best friend, was doing jogo work in the Pelourinho. Every one of the original victims, plus Nelson, had a connection with the jogo do bicho. We had some talking to do the following day. I turned to Anjo.

"Okay, Anj, we've got to track down all three of these guys tomorrow morning and find out what the story is."

"What time should we start?"

"You tell me. What time are these guys likely to be at their posts taking bets?"

"The first drawing is at one o'clock. They will probably be working at ten o'clock."

"Okay, so pick me up at nine thirty. Bones, are you in for making the rounds?"

He nodded and Anjo gave him a hearty pat on the back.

"You are not leaving us yet, Bones."

Bones shrugged.

"Hey, how can I bail out on a lead that was my idea?"

As much as I wanted Bones' idea to work out, at that moment I found myself hoping for the contrary just because I didn't want to have to hear for the rest of my life about how great his idea had been and how it had solved a really difficult case, blah, blah, blah. I wouldn't be able to show my face at any family function without somebody loudly wondering who was the real private investigator in the family. That didn't sound very appealing to me.

I was rolling my eyes in the midst of this thought process when I felt the slightest touch of something against my left hand. Teresa had sidled over behind me and finally gotten my attention. I looked at her and she was whispering something I couldn't quite make out. I leaned towards her and figured out that she was asking me if I wanted to stay at her place that night. I somehow controlled my urge to shout "hell, yes", limiting myself to a slightly lower decibel "oh, yeah". Any illusions of subtlety I had entertained were quickly put to rest by Anjo who asked in a loud voice:

"Should I pick you up tomorrow at the taxi stand or must I come up here to look for you, Mike?"

I glanced at Teresa, who said she had to work the next day. That meant we were rising early, so I told Anjo to meet me at the Hotel do Chile. Both he and Bones gave me their best skeptical looks.

"Cuz, you sure you're gonna be there?"

"I'll be there. Teresa has to work tomorrow, okay?"

With that, my investigative team faded into the night, as did Maria and Josue. That left Teresa and me, with her still lightly touching my left hand. I thought about trying to explain that I hadn't planned on coming up to see her, that it had just happened because of an idea that had occurred to Bones, but my hand worked faster than my brain. It closed around her hand and drew her close to me. We kissed and she led me inside her shack. I didn't really notice what the layout was like because I had eyes for one thing only. I carefully examined every inch of that one thing, taking all the time I needed to commit it to memory. It was the most pleasant memorization task I'd ever forced myself to perform and I finished it way too soon. We both fell asleep instantly when we finished.

It must have been a couple of hours later when I woke up. I had a feeling in my sleep that something wasn't right and I found myself on my back, looking at the undulating tin ceiling. Teresa was next to me in what felt like a pretty sturdy home-made bed, her chest expanding and contracting with each breath. That seemed okay to me. Then I was aware of another sound of breathing, so I propped myself up and looked across the shack to see another small bed on the other side. There wasn't much light, but the shape on top of the bed looked to be about the size of Josue. I figured he must have slipped in sometime after Teresa and I had slipped off, so that seemed okay to me, too. Then I heard something else. It was a very faint noise that started and stopped, then started and stopped again. I turned my head to listen a little better and I realized what I was hearing at about the same time I saw a dark shape move across the floor. It was scurrying. It was also way too big for a mouse, with legs way too short for a cat. That left only one option. It was the biggest fucking rat I had ever seen in my entire New York City life.

I'd ridden the subway all over Manhattan and the other boroughs at the worst hours of the day or night for over twenty years, so I'd seen my fair share of healthy rodents and vermin, both in the tunnels and on the platforms. Hell, some of them had been down there so long, they could even give you directions in between bites of the sandwich or chicken leg they were gnawing on. But in all the drunken, late night, fighting-for-balance hours I'd spent underground waiting for loud public transportation, I'd never seen anything like this. It was the Barry Bonds of rats, impossibly huge and solid-looking, the poster rodent for steroid abuse. All that was missing was a syringe sticking out of its ass. As it moved quickly from side to side, sticking its snout in places where no normal sized rat would dare to go, I couldn't help but wonder why it was moving around so fast. If the eight hundred pound gorilla sleeps wherever he wants, you'd think the ten pound rat could just stroll in search of garbage. There couldn't have been many dogs or cats around that would want a piece of this action, so what was the rush? Who or what was going to bother it? Then it hit me. What if he wasn't the king? What if he wasn't the biggest rat in the neighborhood? That would explain the scurrying. It also explained why I wasn't going to set foot on the floor until the sun was high in the sky, no matter what time Anjo was coming to get me. I lay back down, but I wasn't about to go back to sleep. If the next rat was bigger, I wanted to be able to get as big a head start on my screaming and running as possible.

CHAPTER 44

IN SPITE OF MY nocturnal fears, the next thing I understood was Teresa gently shaking me in the dawn's early light, which wasn't as light as I would have preferred. I couldn't stop myself from looking around the floor before putting my feet down and this earned me a what-in-the-world-are-you-doing-look from Teresa that forced me to explain exactly what in the world I was doing. When I told her I had seen a rat, she flipped the back of her hand at me as if it were the most insignificant thing in the world. When I told her it was a big rat, she asked me how big. When I told her it was the size of a dog, she shook her head with a grin and told me that any rat in her neighborhood would be skinned and eaten before it ever got anywhere near that size. I thought there was at least a slight chance that she wasn't kidding, so I made a mental note never to eat any meat served on a skewer in the immediate area.

I put on my clothes and followed her out to a kind of public latrine, where there were a couple of cabins for taking care of fluid business and a pipe sticking out of a concrete wall that served as a community shower. I had no problem using the cabins, but I wanted no part of the cold water I was sure would come out of the pipe. Teresa was going to shower, but I told her to forget about it, that we'd shower at the Hotel do Chile. If we hustled, she'd have time before she had to be at work and before Anjo showed up at the hotel to put me to work.

We grabbed the rest of our things from inside her shanty and just as we were about to leave, she leaned over and kissed Josue on the forehead as he lay in bed. I assumed he'd stay there until such a time when the rats, even the big ones, wouldn't dare show their faces. It was still pretty dark when we stepped outside, so Teresa took me by the hand and made sure I didn't kill myself on the way down to the road. She led me to a bus stop, but in the interest of time I made her follow me to the taxi stand. She didn't object when I made the point that a hot bath was in her future if we could make it to the hotel in time.

Traffic was light, so the return trip to Chile Street was even faster than our trip out the night before. It was only six-fifteen when I opened the door to my room and it was only about six-seventeen when I was lying naked next to Teresa. I couldn't think of a better way to start the day and I didn't even try. Afterward I just watched her soak in the bathtub, enjoying every second of being in the luxurious no-star Hotel do Chile bathroom.

It wasn't long before she had to get up and go to work and when she did, the room didn't seem so interesting anymore. It was seven-fifteen and I needed to do some thinking before Anjo showed up, so I decided to walk over to the park near the Lacerda Elevator.

The city was starting to wake up. A few cars were on the street, taxis were starting to circulate and the early morning workforce was already into the first part of its day. I bought a cafezinho in a paper cup from a street vendor and sat on one of the benches in the park, watching the world pass. I was planning my itinerary from the Pelourinho down to the lighthouse area in Barra, when I became aware of somebody beside me. I don't know how it happened that I hadn't noticed anybody come over, but there was Wanda Miranda, flashing me a smile usually reserved for restaurant clients only. She had a makeshift table and a bag of what I guessed were still the best pastries in all of Salvador under her arm.

"Bom dia, Mike Breza. Como vai?"

"Tudo bem, Dona Wanda. E voce?"

She nodded at me in approval of my improving Portuguese, then asked me how my night had been. When I told her it had been okay, she said she was glad to hear it because night was usually when the big rats came out. The sight of my uvula hanging from the roof of my wide open mouth must have been pretty funny because she burst into laughter before explaining that she had crossed paths with Teresa as the two of them were on their way to their respective jobs. I was relieved to hear that the explanation for her knowing my nocturnal business was somewhat less than supernatural. I also accepted the pastry she offered me in apology for almost spraining my neck by yanking my chain so hard. The pastry went so well with my cafezinho that I tried to give her some money, which she refused. I told her I had to meet up with Anjo and she wished me luck with the rest of my day. She also told me to come visit her at the end of the day if I had a hankering for another pastry. Somehow I knew I'd be back. She probably did, too.

It was nine-twenty when I got back to the hotel. Bones and Anjo were already waiting for me, sipping a cafezinho at the reception desk with João. In contrast with Wanda Miranda, João seemed to be ignorant about my previous night's activities, a first since my arrival in Salvador. There was probably a supernatural explanation for it, but I decided not to pursue the issue.

"Bom dia, Anjo, como vai? Bom dia, Cuz."

"Good morning to you, Mike. Are you ready to work?"

"After a street cafezinho and a pastry from Wanda Miranda, I'm ready for anything. Where to first?"

"The Pelourinho to see Paulo Amado."

"It's your town, Anjo. Lead the way."

The three of us hustled off past the cathedral and down to the Largo do Pelourinho, where Anjo stopped to get his bearings. It didn't take very long and five minutes later we were milling around with all the potential winners in the upcoming one o'clock drawing. Anjo tapped one of the guys taking bets on the shoulder. It was Paulo Amado, Carlos de Souza's best buddy. He didn't act surprised to see Anjo, even though it couldn't have been an everyday occurrence, and he was real friendly to Bones and me, extending his hand with a smile. Anjo asked for a word in private, so the three of us stepped around the corner onto Tabuão Street. Paulo asked Anjo what was up and Anjo explained that we had some questions relating to Carlos de Souza's death. This didn't seem to faze Paulo in the least. His hang-loose posture against the wall said we should fire away.

I explained that Anjo would translate the questions because I didn't trust my Portuguese in such a delicate situation. The first thing I wanted to know was if there had been any police activity out of the ordinary around his turf lately. As soon as I said the word police, Paulo's hang-loose posture was a thing of the past. No language barrier there. His back straightened right up, he shifted from foot to foot and tried to find something other than us to look at. I glanced over at Bones and Anjo.

"I don't need any more answer than that. How 'bout you guys?"

They both shook their heads and Bones spoke up.

"Nah, we might want to get some details, though."

Anjo was way ahead of us. He put his hand on Paulo's shoulder, applying enough pressure to convince him to stand still so he could whisper in his ear. I could make out that Anjo was telling him how important it was that he tell us whatever he could. Anjo also made the point that he would consider it a personal favor if Paulo helped out. With the pressure he was applying to Paulo's shoulder, Anjo didn't have to say how he'd view the opposite.

Anjo's street cred carried the day as Paulo became a broken dike of explanations. I couldn't follow everything he was saying and I noticed that even Bones was struggling to keep up, but it was pretty obvious that something unusual had been going on with the jogo. It was also pretty obvious that it made Paulo really nervous. He practically begged Anjo to keep his name out of it. If it hadn't been for Anjo's hand on his shoulder, he might've left town right then and there. Anjo listened until Paulo ran out of words and pleas. Then he gave his word that Paulo could count on him to keep quiet. This was enough to calm Paulo almost instantly, earning Anjo additional street cred points, as if he needed any. Anjo took his hand off the guy's shoulder and Paulo went back to taking numbers as fast as he could without betraying how nervous he'd just felt. Anjo started moving away and jerked his head at us to follow him. When we were half a block away from the betting action, Anjo slowed down. I couldn't wait any longer.

"Anj, what'd he say?"

Anjo took a deep breath.

"Paulo says that there is a disagreement over the jogo in some parts of Salvador."

"What kind of disagreement? "

"Something with the police."

"What, the cops are finally cracking down on the jogo?"

Anjo shook his head.

"No, it is a disagreement among the police over who will control the jogo in certain parts of the city. The ones who have been in charge for a long time are being pressured by other police. These new police want the jogo's payments to the police to go through them and they are trying to convince the cambistas to pass them the money instead of giving it to the old police contacts. Paulo is sure that Carlos was murdered as a warning to the cambista here of what could happen…"

"…if he didn't play ball with the new kids on the block. So who's Carlos' boss giving the money to these days?"

"The new police. The old ones never killed anyone."

"That's probably a good career move. So how long has he been making payments to the new guys?"

"Since the day they found Carlos on the church steps."

"Does he know who these new guys are?"

Anjo shook his head.

It made sense to me, but Bones had a question.

"So why didn't this guy Paulo tell somebody what was going on?"

Anjo looked at him.

"Bones, there is no one to tell."

"What about another cop? A clean one?"

Anjo shook his head again.

"No, Bones, you cannot tell the good from the bad like in the cinema. They all wear the same uniform."

"What about telling his bosses in the jogo?"

"They know, but they must work through their own contacts in the police. They cannot force other police to do anything."

"So the old police contacts have to take care of these new guys?"

He nodded and turned away.

"Come on, we have other people to speak with."

Next on the visiting list was Jorge Arruda's half-brother, Armando. He supposedly worked for a cambista down near the lighthouse in the Barra area of the city. We cut back across the Praça da Se to reach Anjo's taxi in front of the hotel. From there we headed south on the 7th of September Avenue and ran into hellish traffic right around the lighthouse. That gave Anjo the chance to show off his taxi-driver chops. He started making rights

and lefts on streets, paths and sidewalks like it was his last
time behind the wheel. I think we even drove through
somebody's living room just before Anjo invented a
parking spot around the corner from the lighthouse on
Oceanic Avenue. It was urban driving as performance art
and we had been treated to a masterpiece. As we got out
of the car, Bones and I gave Anjo the applause he had
earned. He took a well-deserved bow.

"Holy shit, Anj, that was spectacular."

"Anjo, anytime you want to come back to New York,
you've got a job waiting for you."

"Thank you, Mike, but I will stay where I am. Let's
go."

We walked east on Oceanic Avenue and it was very
well named. Even the old sea dog Bones was impressed.
A series of beaches stretched eastward as far as the eye
could see. I was just starting to daydream about a day
with Teresa at one of them when we hit the corner of
Centenario Avenue. It was one of those corners that
everyone back in New York City would have described
as "bustling". People were streaming in very direction,
yakking away on cellphones and to other pedestrians,
often at the same time. I didn't see many Blackberries,
but they were bound to show up sooner or later. There
was some kind of shopping center or mall up Centenario
Avenue from where we stood, so in addition to all the
pedestrians not watching where they were going, there
were tons of vehicles being piloted by people guilty of
driving while dialing. It was utter chaos, but it was a very
Brazilian chaos, which meant that everybody seemed to
find their way to the other side of where they were going

with nobody losing their lives or their cool. No one even bumped into us.

In the midst of all the movement, Anjo managed to zero in on the newspaper stand just around the corner. It was nothing special to look at, four walls and a roof slapped together with barely enough room inside for a man and his dirty thoughts. There were a couple of doors that swung open like a flasher to reveal every skin magazine and tabloid published south of the Panama Canal. You could get cigarettes, both packs and loosies, you could get candy, some of it even made in the last five years, you could get gum, snacks, sodas, beer and all the gossip you wanted. But the sidewalk bustle in front of the stand was no match for the steady line of people doing business in back. That's where the real action was. It was high noon, so people were anxious about getting their bets in for the one o'clock drawing.

Anjo stepped around back with Bones and me right behind him. There were three guys writing down numbers and taking money. All three were seated on makeshift furniture that ranged from a bucket to something that had probably been a real chair at one time in its career. There was a fourth guy leaning against the back of the news stand that would pick up the money and papers from the three scribes every five minutes or so. I made him as the cambista, the guy who was responsible in the eyes of the people who ran the jogo. That meant Armando had to be one of the three guys sitting down. Since two of them were black, I figured that the third guy, a coffee-colored dude with tight curly hair, had to be Armando because Jorge Arruda, the victim, had been a tan-skinned cadaver. Of course, it being Brazil, I was dead wrong. Anjo went up to the darker-skinned of the two black guys and whispered something in his ear. The guy didn't even look up from his work. He nodded and called over the boss. The boss listened to Anjo for a second, shook his hand, made a reverential head bow and took the black man's place on the bucket fielding customers. Anjo and his new buddy walked back over to where Bones and I were standing.

He introduced us to Armando Arruda, a thin, five-foot-nine inch black man with incipient dreadlocks, bright dark eyes and a wispy goatee. He was dressed in denim shorts, a Bob Marley t-shirt and flip-flops. We shook hands and he looked us right in the eye while demonstrating an iron grip. Anjo explained what the story was, who we were and what we wanted to know. Unlike Paulo Amado, this guy never looked away. He spoke slowly in a low voice, measuring his words carefully so that even I understood what he said.

It was almost a carbon copy of what we'd already heard from Paulo Amado, internal bickering among the police over the jogo's spoils. According to Armando, the newcomers wanted more than their fair share; they wanted total control and weren't averse to killing people to get it. Since it was easier to kill unarmed people than other law enforcement officers and since it didn't make any sense to kill the guys who actually made the money, the early victims of the power struggle had been relatives of the jogo's workers. As soon as Armando had heard about his half-brother's death, he'd known it was a warning to all of them working the Centenario Avenue spot. His boss, Kingston, knew it as well and had started turning over his money to the newcomers. It had caused some issues with the jogo's owners, but Kingston's view was that they had to settle it with their own police contacts. Since Kingston was still alive and working a couple of weeks later, the strategy seemed to be sound. At that point I nudged Anjo.

"Ask him if he knows who the new cops are."

When Anjo relayed the question, Armando said he had seen the guys come and collect the money, but didn't know their names. But he knew for sure that they worked out of the headquarters on Alfredo de Brito Street.

"How does he know that, Anj?"

"He lives over there and has seen them going in and out of the building."

"Can he describe them?"

The answer was somewhat less than helpful.

"He says they looked like cops. They had sunglasses, badges and guns, which they weren't timid about showing."

"Can he at least tell us what color they were?"

"Not black."

Armando's whole story took about ten minutes. In that time, the betting lines for the jogos had only increased, so Armando had to jump back to work, letting Kingston get back to supervising the money. We thanked Armando for his time and Anjo swore to him that he wouldn't tell anybody what had been said. Armando smiled and told Anjo not to worry about it, that he was a big boy and took responsibility for his own words. We made sure to thank Kingston for his help as well. He told us it was nothing, but wanted to know if I was the guy who had won two straight days betting the turkey. I told him I was and he insisted on shaking my hand to see if some of my luck would rub off on him.

CHAPTER 45

WE MADE OUR WAY back to Anjo's taxi and he performed another routine miracle by getting us out of the Barra traffic and onto the 7th of September Avenue, heading north toward Bonfim Church. As I checked out the scenery flowing by, I remembered the question I wanted to ask Anjo.

"So, Anj, when we went around back of the news stand and saw the guys working the numbers, I thought for sure the light-skinned guy was Armando since Jorge Arruda looked pretty much like that in the pictures I saw. How is it that his half-brother is so much darker?"

That earned me another of those what-an-ignorant-gringo-tourist looks from Anjo, although this one only lasted a second.

"I cannot really say, Mike. Here in Brazil, at least in Salvador, many relatives from the same family are different shades of black, brown and white. Armando and Jorge shared the same father and last name, but had different mothers. Perhaps Armando's mother is a mulata or a black woman. But even if she is, it is still impossible to know what color a child will be in Salvador unless the man and woman are purely of one race or another. And that can be difficult to find in this city, where all the races are mixed together so completely."

Bones joined in.

"It's a strange place for racism to exist."

Anjo's rejoinder was a hard truth.

"But it does and I live it every day."

We rode the rest of the way in silence.

It was just one o'clock when we arrived at Bonfim Church in search of Patricio Teixeira, cousin of Flavio Guimarães. Anjo parked his rig at a taxi stand by the church. Even though the only directions we had were "somewhere near the Bonfim Church", it wasn't too hard to figure out where the local cambista spot was. The first drawing of the day must have just taken place, so Bones and I followed Anjo who followed the flow of the crowd to Caiena Frio Street near the church. The news, mostly bad for most of the players and great for a selected few, was already out, so most of the crowd was milling about talking about what animal they should have played, but in reality never would have. It was like a very subdued block party that took place three times a day. Anjo sussed out who the cambista was and asked him for Patricio Teixeira. There was no curveball here in terms of Patricio's skin color, as he was the same shade of brown that I'd seen in the pictures of Flavio. He was tall, about six foot three, and skinny enough that his pants looked to be losing their struggle against gravity. Or maybe New

York hip-hop fashion had made its way to Salvador. It was hard to tell.

Anjo introduced himself and us, then told our story. Patricio was a little wary of talking in a crowd, so we moved up the block to a coffee stand for a round of cafezinhos. After the first two sips, Patricio pretty much repeated what we had already heard twice. Some cops they hadn't seen before had come around claiming things had changed, giving them new instructions for turning over the money. The head of the Bonfim operation, a guy named Ribeiro, had checked with the powers and found out that it wasn't true. The cops came by twice more to warn them and then Flavio had turned up dead on the church steps. Nobody associated with the jogo had been fooled by the racist overtones of the murder, but none of them had said anything to the press either, for fear of being the next victim. Ribeiro, who knew Flavio through Patricio, had been convinced and had started turning over a portion of his money to the new cops. He had let his bosses know what was going on, but so far, there had been no reaction to the new pressure being applied at street level. At that point I interrupted.

"Anj, ask him if he knows who the cops were or what headquarters they work out of."

Anjo put the question to him, but Patricio had no idea. But he did give a fast answer about something we hadn't asked and it was information that got Anjo's attention.

"What did he say, Anj?"

"He overheard the new cops talking as they left after collecting the money and one said the plan of the delegado was starting to give results."

"Who's the delegado?"

"Patricio claims he heard the name Delegado Neto."

I looked at Patricio, who nodded his confirmation. That's when it hit me. I turned to Anjo.

"Anj, didn't you tell me that the priests of the Passo Street Church were the only ones who had the keys to the gates around the stairs where the dead bodies were found?"

"Yes, because it is true. They are the only ones with the keys. They open the gates an hour beore Mass starts."

"But the morning Nelson's body was found, Delegado Neto and his squad showed up and opened the gate to retrieve the body. They must have keys, too."

"Maybe they got them from the priests."

"It doesn't matter where they got them. The point is they have them, which means access to the steps for easy disposal of bodies. We already know Neto is obsessed with the jogo do bicho, supposedly because he wants to clean it up, and he spent the whole time he was talking to me doodling swastikas on his fucking notepad. Add this to the fact that one of the jogo guys overheard two police collection agents, new guys never seen on a collection route before, talking about how Neto's plan was working. Jesus, what conclusion jumps out at you?"

Nobody said a word, so I said it for them.

"The whole fucking case is about Delegado Antonio Neto making a power play to take over the jogo do bicho in Salvador. Or at least certain parts of it. He had all these guys killed and set up the bodies to look like racist hate crimes, knowing the cambistas would understand the real message and not be able to rat him out. He also knew that the papers would pick up the racism angle and trumpet it for all it was worth."

I looked at Anjo.

"This means that Nelson's death wasn't a mistake by some dumb ass cops acting on their own. It's really part of the pattern!"

Patricio didn't understand any of my rant, but Bones' expression, mouth agape, reflected exactly how I felt. After a couple of seconds delay, we thanked Patricio for his help and let him wander back to the mill-around so he could start work for the second drawing in three hours. We walked back to the taxi stand near the church. As we climbed into the car, Bones spoke first.

"Okay, now what?"

I gave him the only answer I had.

"Fuck if I know, man."

From where I sat, we had a whole big pile of shit. The idea of talking to the victims' family and friends involved in the jogo had worked spectacularly well, giving us a very plausible scenario, maybe even the correct explanation, for why the four victims had been murdered and dumped on the church steps. The problem was, even if we were right, there was absolutely nothing we could do about it. If it really was a scheme cooked up by a bunch of bad cops, a couple of foreigners and a pai de santo couldn't go up against the Brazilian Federal Police without winding up in a ditch somewhere covered with flies. And with Delegado Neto as the brains behind the scheme, the likely forecast was heavy pain prior to the ditch nap. Anjo pulled out of his makeshift parking space, leaned on his horn, then leaned on his New York vocabulary to ask the New York version of Bones' prior question.

"Okay, so what the fuck do we do now?"

Nothing had changed.

"Fuck if I know, man."

Bones spoke up.

"So, Anj, there's no way we can go after Delegado Neto, is there?"

"I don't see any way to do this. We would need very good friends in the Federal Police and they would also have to believe our story."

I chimed in.

"Yeah, that sounds like two strikes against us from the get-go."

"Not to mention that we don't have any real evidence that Delegado Neto is behind all of this."

"Bones, how much proof do we need? All of the victims' relatives say there's a power play on the police force for control of the jogo do bicho and one of them overheard the bag men talking about Neto. Not only that, Neto was watching the local cambista like a hawk, he told me he was going to clean up the jogo in Salvador and that he was going to be ruthless about it. What else do I need to know?"

"Come on, Mikey! The closest I've ever gotten to a courtroom is repeats of Law & Order, but even I can tell you that all that shit you cited is just circumstantial. If it couldn't pass muster in a U.S. court, which is supposedly somewhat impartial at least some of the time, how are you gonna convict a cop, a high-ranking cop no less, in Brazil with crap evidence like that?"

He had a good point.

"Bones, I know you're right, but it just sticks in my craw that this asshole is getting away with this shit."

It was Anjo's turn to talk sense.

"I agree with both of you, but I must tell you that the most important thing you have said, in my opinion, is 'get away'."

I didn't understand.

"What do you mean, Anj?"

He took a deep breath and exhaled before answering.

"We have spoken to three jogo employees of three different cambistas in three different parts of the city today. Two Americans and a Brazilian working together like this will get somebody's attention. That somebody is going to tell the police something and the police trying to take over the jogo are going to find out. These people do not seem to me to be the type of people that are willing to take chances. That means the three of us have to be very careful. For you two, I think that means leaving Salvador and possibly Brazil as soon as possible."

It sounded like a worst case scenario.

"You mean leave right now? "

He nodded.

"How long do you think it will take for Delegado Neto and the boys to react?"

"It could be two days, it could be a matter of hours, but I assure you that they will react."

"What about you, Anj?"

"I cannot leave Brazil, certainly, and I don't want to leave Salvador. I can disappear for a while until the problem is resolved."

"How does it get resolved, Anj?"

"I do not know, Mike, but it cannot last forever. One group of the police or the other must win, no? When that happens, what we think we know will not be a threat to them."

His logic was flawed with regard to his own safety. I didn't think there was any way Delegado Neto would let him off the hook, but he was probably right about me and Bones. We needed to get out of town and the sooner, the better. I looked at Bones.

"Anjo's probably right, Cuz. I can get my stuff at the hotel and head right out to the airport to catch the next flight to anywhere. How fast can you get out on your boat?"

"I can be ready to sail in a couple of hours, but I won't be able to go home just yet. I can probably make it up to Belem or Fortaleza for a quick layover to get real supplies and then take off for home, but hold on a second. You shouldn't go to the airport. You should come with me and just get the hell out of town. You can get a plane from Fortaleza or Belem. This way Neto can't touch you."

As much as I hated sailing, I hated being in a ditch covered with flies more. His idea made sense. Then it occurred to me that it might make sense for Anjo as well.

"Hey, Anj, maybe you should come on the boat, too. That way you wouldn't have to lay low in Neto's town. What do you think?"

"I have never been to Belem or Fortaleza. Maybe it is time. Can I go on the boat, Bones?"

"Hey, the more the merrier. Just don't puke on the newly painted deck."

"What about a crew?"

"I can get us up the coast by myself with no problem, as long as you two clowns don't get in the way. I'll find somebody up north to help me get back to Florida. And maybe a couple of the dock guys from here are willing to do the whole trip. I'll ask as soon as I get to the boat."

As he pulled into the Modelo Market area, Anjo said he'd go pick up a few things and meet us down at the boat. I had to grab my stuff from the hotel and settle the bill before going to the dock. Bones would go right to the Sweet St. Pete and get everything ready. We wished each other good luck and went our separate ways.

CHAPTER 46

I WAS NERVOUS AS I walked back down Misericordia Street toward Chile Street. My nervousness turned to surprise when I reached the corner of Das Vassouras Street and practically knocked over a standing tray of desserts belonging to Wanda Miranda. The bigger surprise was that Detective Santos, sidekick to Delegado Neto, was standing next to her munching on a pastry. I heard the faint buzzing of flies in my head.

"Oy, Mike Breza, como vai? Tudo bem?"

Everything wasn't good and it was looking to get worse. The only positive thing I could think of was that I didn't see any black sedans nearby. I tried to act natural by telling her everything was great and went to shake her hand, but she gave me a kiss on both cheeks and introduced me to Detective Santos.

"Mike Breza, you know the Detective Santos? He good man."

I extended my hand. Detective Santos shook it after cleaning his.

"We've met before, Wanda, and you know it. Como vai, Detective?"

Santos mumbled something and finished his pastry while Wanda spoke.

"The Detective Santos is very good man. I know him since he is very little because his mother my good friend."

"Really? Is that right, Detective Santos?"

My nervousness was fading as an idea took shape in my head. Maybe I could play dumb and gain some time.

"So, Detective Santos, any progress on that murder case?"

He explained to me in Portuguese that he couldn't comment about an ongoing investigation. It was answer number twenty-three, straight from the Detective's Public Relations Handbook. He was nervous in giving me the answer and I got another bad idea that I couldn't resist. I told him in Portuguese that I certainly understood that he couldn't say anything about the case. Then I hit him with another question.

"Any progress in cleaning up the jogo do bicho like Delegado Neto said he wanted to do?"

Santos looked at me like I was Shango himself, ready to smite him. He was either a great actor or he was more nervous than ever. I couldn't control myself.

"Did you ever consider the possibility that there might be some connection between the jogo do bicho and the murders? Just an idea, seeing as how the jogo's an illegal business and there might be real criminals involved in it."

Out of the corner of my eye I could see that Wanda Miranda was smiling at Santos, nodding her head. That made me nervous and I stopped myself from further digging my own grave. What the fuck was I thinking, running my mouth to Delegado Neto's lapdog like that? Bones was right, I needed to get some self-control therapy or something.

Detective Santos had finished his pastry and turned around to leave, increasing my desire to sprint for the Hotel do Chile as fast as I could. I turned to Wanda.

"Look, Wanda, I'm in deep trouble and I'm leaving Salvador right now. Unless by some miracle Teresa is waiting for me at the hotel, I won't be able to see her to say good-bye. Please tell her for me that it was an emergency, a matter of life and death. My own."

She nodded, but had other questions on her mind.

"You like Detective Santos, no? He is a good man. You will see."

"Whatever you say, Wanda. Just promise me you'll talk to Teresa for me."

"Eu prometo."

I gave her a kiss and thanked her, then left her in the dust as I hustled off to the hotel. It wasn't my day for miracles, so Teresa wasn't there waiting for me. There was nobody at the front desk either, so I just went straight up to my room. I swept all my non-clothing into the backpack, stuffed my clothes on top and crammed my notebook and pen into the outside pocket. I closed up and went downstairs to pay the bill.

João was on duty at the reception desk and for the second time since I had arrived in Salvador, he appeared to have no clue as to what I was doing.

"Oy, Mike, you checking out?"

"Yeah, João, and I'm in a bit of a hurry."

"What's the rush?"

"That's a story for another day, my friend. Let's just say my glass is out of sand. Listen, I need a favor from you."

He was printing up the paper work for me to sign.

"I'm listening."

"If you see Teresa, please explain that I had to get the hell out of here in a hurry and I didn't have time to find her to say good-bye."

He put the papers on the counter in front of me.

"I got it. It's Neto, right?"

"Could be, man. Will you talk to Teresa for me?"

"Of course I will, brother. Good luck."

I signed the papers, he gave me the Brazilian soul shake and I was out the door. I made myself walk slowly, trying not to attract unnecessary attention or betray my rising panic. I got on the Lacerda Elevator with everybody else going to the lower city and audibly exhaled with relief. I stepped out onto Conceição da Praia Street for the last time and almost walked into Anjo.

"Oy, Mike!"

"Anjo, great timing, let's get over to the Sweet St. Pete."

We walked at a steady, not-guilty-of-anything pace past the Plaza Cayru and Wanda Miranda's place of employment and onto Belgica Street. We were only a couple of blocks from the docks when everything went south. Out of the corner of my eye I noticed a black sedan with tinted windows just behind us, rolling at the same pace we were walking. Anjo saw it, too, but neither of us turned our heads.

"Okay, Anj, it's your town. What do we do?"

"We keep walking like nothing is happening. If we run, we'll be shot down in the street like dogs."

A second black sedan pushed my adrenaline to the maximum by cutting around the car following us and screeching to a halt on the sidewalk, cutting off our advance. All four doors opened and five unfriendly-looking men got out of the car. They all made a point of showing they had guns strapped on their shoulders or their waist. The slow-moving sedan pulled even with us by the curb and both back doors opened, revealing none other than Delegado Neto and another unfriendly cop, both of whom stepped up on the curb next to us. That made six unfriendly police thugs plus Delegado Neto. Even without Detective Santos, the odds for us were less than good.

The two of us were frozen in place and it was a bad place to be. I whispered to Anjo.

"It was nice working with you, man."

Before he could answer, Delegado Neto was sneering in my face.

"Senhor Breza, nice to see you again."

I tried to answer, but he closed my mouth with the back of his hand. It was probably for the better. I reached up to wipe off whatever was dripping from my chin and he grabbed my wrist.

"Oy, what is this? A ribbon from the Igreja do Bonfim?"

He turned to Unfriendly Police Thug Number Six and demanded a knife. It didn't surprise me that the assistant gave Neto a choice of two. Delegado Neto grabbed the larger one, another detail that didn't surprise me, and clicked it open. It looked sharp. He then grabbed my wrist and slipped the knife blade in between my wrist and the ribbon, slicing it like a man with extensive experience in wielding a blade. The ribbon fluttered to the ground. He gave the knife back to its owner and smiled at me.

"Mr. Breza, I think your Bonfim wishes will not be coming true."

He went to tag me with a roundhouse right hand and my bar fight instincts led me to do exactly the wrong thing by blocking it. He let himself wide open for an uppercut with that move and I knew Jimmy Keane would have been proud of me for realizing it, but I got my instincts back under control and didn't hit him. What I couldn't control was the blindside punch to my head from Neto's assistant that laid me out on the ground. That didn't work out so well for him because Anjo gave him two lightning capoeira kicks, one squarely in the balls and the second in the face, leaving the poor sap writhing on the ground. The applause for that combination consisted of a series of clicks of handguns being cocked and aimed at us. Anjo raised his hands above his head, but I had to use mine to hold the ribs where Neto had just kicked me. The ditch with the flies didn't seem so bad at that moment. At least I'd be lying down with nobody hitting me. Delegado Neto, however, seemed to be enjoying himself.

"This has been fun, Mr. Breza, but it's time for us to get to work. Please get up and get in the car. You and your friend are under arrest."

I could breathe just enough to croak out a couple of words.

"What's the charge?"

Delegado Neto looked at me with pity.

"I don't need a charge, Mr. Breza, I'm the delegado for this district. You disobeyed a direct order from me to stay away from the jogo do bicho, which you know is an illegal activity. You went around my city talking to cambistas and you shouldn't have done that. So please get up, I don't want to kick you again. I want you to be awake for our little talk."

I couldn't resist the temptation.

"Does the talk take place on the steps of Santissimo Sacramento Church or is that just where I end up?"

That earned me another kick to the ribs and one to the head for good measure. Neither kick hurt as much as being yanked to my knees by a couple of the unfriendlies, who also slapped the bracelets on me, then jerked me all the way up to my feet. My right eye was starting to swell, but I could still see that Anjo had matching jewelry on his wrists. I also saw a number of new cars joining the party. I counted four more black sedans, each of which spewed forth at least four well-armed men, along with two regular cop cars and a large van. A bunch of riot cops streamed out of the van and lined up in front of Delegado Neto's car, preventing us from getting in. I looked at Anjo as best as I could, but he didn't know what was playing either.

Then a large man with a very expensive suit, sunglasses to match and an air of command got out of one of the sedans and walked over to the six unfriendlies that had come in with Delegado Neto. He said something to the five of them that were standing and they holstered their weapons. The sixth guy was still on the ground, but the boss leaned over and offered him his handkerchief to wipe the blood off his face. That made the guy feel better and he managed to get to his feet. The boss man then stood next to the original unfriendlies with his hands clasped in front of him.

The only guy more confused than me was Delegado Neto. He watched the whole scene unfold with his mouth wide open and an agitated look on his face. He apparently knew the guy in charge of the muscle because he asked him what was going on and called him by his name, Sergio. He didn't get much of an answer, adding to the overall sense of confusion.

At that moment, another black sedan pulled up. Everybody turned to see Detective Santos step out. Delegado Neto's expression was one of relief as Santos strode toward him. He even managed a smile as Santos got close to speak to him. The smile faded quickly as Santos spoke, replaced by a grim, hard look. None of us could hear Santos, but we didn't have to. Whatever Santos said was bad news for Neto, who for a second tensed his body as if he was going to do something physical. I wasn't the only one who noticed it and the riot cops took one step toward Neto, who immediately relaxed. Santos reached underneath Neto's sport coat and pulled out a handgun. He then leaned down and took a smaller gun from an ankle strap on Neto's right leg.

The boss of the muscle directed two of his guys to escort Neto to the back seat of one of the black sedans. Neto sat in between the enforcers and one of them produced a pair of handcuffs that seemed destined for Delegado Neto's wrists once they were out of public view.

The rest of the supporting cast started to slip away as well, filing back to the vehicles they'd arrived in. The muscle boss undid my cuffs, then did the same favor for Anjo. It looked like the two of them knew each other because they exchanged the slightest of nods as Anjo rubbed his wrists. In less than five minutes the only people left standing were Anjo, Detective Santos and me. There was somebody else in the car that had brought Santos, but I wasn't about to try and see who it was. Detective Santos called us over. His English was much better than I expected.

"Gentlemen, I apologize for what happened. It would be better for everyone if you didn't talk about it."

He didn't have to tell us twice. For starters, neither Anjo nor I was very sure of what we had just seen. Also, the pain in my ribs told me it wasn't the moment to disobey a direct police request.

"Mr. Breza, please stay away from the jogo do bicho from now on and enjoy the rest of your visit to Brazil."

Given the performance we'd just seen, it seemed like sound advice.

"I'll do that, Detective Santos. Thank you very much."

I extended my hand, as did Anjo, and he shook them both before turning to leave. He stopped just before he got to the car and looked back.

"Oh, one more thing, it's Delegado Santos now, not Detective."

With that, he was gone. I looked down at my feet and saw my Bonfim Church ribbon lying where it had landed. I picked it up and stuffed it in my pocket. The act wasn't lost on Anjo, who grinned.

"So, Mike, how are your wishes turning out?"

"So far, so, good, Anj, so far, so good."

"A ribbon from Bonfim can be useful, no? Especially when it comes from Wanda Miranda."

"My thoughts exactly, Anjo."

I touched the figa hanging around my neck as I answered.

CHAPTER 47

WE LIMPED OVER TO the Sweet St. Pete, where Bones couldn't believe his ears, but was relieved that he didn't have to make a run for it with two inept sailors on board. He claimed the boat carried enough dead weight as it was. He also said I looked like shit and should see a doctor. We left him to revel in his new-found freedom and went straight to the nearest emergency room, where they told me I had a couple of bruised, possibly cracked ribs, a swollen eye with a footprint on it and a two kick headache. They also told me they'd seen worse, gave me some painkillers and told me to go sleep it off. João hadn't rented out my room yet, so I managed to install myself back in the Hotel do Chile at about eight-thirty. Anjo made sure I got upstairs, then promised me he'd be by in the morning for breakfast.

I woke up at about four in the morning, feeling a little disoriented. I looked to my right and thought I must have been dreaming. It was Teresa Cardoso, in all her naked glory, sleeping next to me. My ribs and head still hurt, but not quite so much when I looked at her. I was feeling pretty lucky as I drifted back off to sleep.

The next morning, it was me that needed the hot bath to soak my aching body. Being Saturday, Teresa was off from work and stayed with me, making the period of time before the bath even more enjoyable than the water, although I was somewhat limited in my movements. It didn't seem to matter much. She'd received messages at work from both Wanda and João about my fleeing the country and she'd gone home the previous night feeling sad and angry. Then Anjo had shown up at nine-thirty to tell her about our encounter with the police. He'd offered her a ride to the hotel, which she had accepted. The rest was more good luck for me. I liked the feel of her hands on my arm as I stepped out of the tub. It felt like something I could get used to.

Anjo knocked on the door at a little after nine o'clock, just like he'd promised the night before. Both Teresa and I were already dressed and ready to eat. At least I was. There's nothing like a good old-fashioned ass-kicking to build up an appetite. We went downstairs to the first class dining room of the Hotel do Chile. João saw us exit the elevator and ditched the front desk to join us for a cafezinho or two. We ordered a fairly extensive breakfast, then sipped our coffee. Everybody was all smiles, nobody more than me.

Anjo had brought the newspapers, but instead of front page tabloid news, our run-in with tons of police on Belgica Street in broad daylight in which one cop had apparently been detained by some of his own colleagues didn't even make the fine print in the classifieds. News of the incident was nowhere to be found. I guess freedom of the press also meant freedom to not publish stories that would put authorities on both sides of the law in a foul mood. It was probably a good career move for all the reporters and editors involved.

Fortunately for my insatiable curiosity, Anjo had already spoken with the new cambista over at Nelson's old news stand, a guy named Bruno, who had told him that it was business as usual. Deliveries were to be made through the normal channels, and, yeah, he'd heard about pressures from some new cops, but that had pretty much gone away. He didn't know why. It didn't seem too hard to read between the lines, but I wanted to be sure.

"So, Anj, what do you make of this? What happened to Delegado Neto? Are we done? Is the case finished?"

The food arrived at that moment and Anjo delayed his answer with a big bite of toast. It seemed like a good idea to the rest of us as well. Then he spoke.

"I do not know what has happened with Delegado Neto. I can only say that he will have much less authority in the police department from now on, if he has any at all."

"Is there any chance he's lying in a ditch somewhere covered with flies?"

Anjo shook his head.

"If he is dead, I don't think there is any chance his body is above ground."

"How do we find out if he's dead or not?"

Anjo shook his head again.

"We don't. You are alive, I am alive, Bones is alive and that is enough. The message is clear."

"And that message is?"

"Police justice is a police matter. It is not for ordinary people like us."

"Okay, so what do we say to the victims' wives?"

"What do you think we should say?"

"That we think the murderer was picked up by the police and they're handling it with no press coverage. That's all we can really do."

"I agree. We can talk to the widows this afternoon and this evening, if you are able to walk."

That sounded like a good plan, but not as good as finishing our breakfast. While we were eating, João pressed for some details about what had happened, but neither Anjo nor I were talking. We liked breathing too much. When we finished, I suggested that we check in with Bones to see if he was still intent on sailing north sooner rather than later.

Anjo, Teresa and I wound our way over to the Lacerda Elevator, then down to the lower city. Anjo and I exchanged glances as we walked past the place the cops had stopped us the day before and I found myself checking around for black sedans. Teresa noticed what I was doing and squeezed my arm.

"Não se preocupe, não tem carros pretos, meu bem."

She was right, there were no black cars in sight, but it was probably going to be a while before I felt comfortable walking down Belgica Street.

Bones was up and moving about his boat like a man with someplace to go when we arrived. He grinned from ear to ear when he saw us and hopped down to the dock.

"Hey, you guys survived the night. Bom dia, Teresa."

"Bom dia, seu Bones."

Bones gave all of a us a firm hug, although he was considerably more gentle with my ribs than Anjo's and Teresa's.

"I'm glad you guys came down. You saved me the trouble of having to come up to say good-bye."

That answered the question I had on his departure, but I asked it anyway.

"Are you taking off today?"

"Today is the day, Cuz. Since I scrambled like crazy yesterday, I've got everything ready to go, so I'm not going to waste the effort."

"Are you going straight home?"

He shook his head.

"Nah, I'm gonna go to Fortaleza and Belem before making the big jump home. It seemed like a good idea yesterday, so why not?"

"What about a crew?"

"I've got a couple of guys who'll go with me to Belem and maybe all the way. They'll see St. Pete Beach, then come back home to Salvador by plane."

"Sounds like a plan. When do you leave?"

"Now that I've seen you guys, in about an hour."

"Holy shit, so soon?"

"Hey, Fortaleza is a long way off, my friend."

"Wow, well, listen, man, thanks for all the help. Your big idea put us on the right track."

"It also got you your ass kicked in the street."

"Yeah, well, nothing new there. See you back in the States?"

"No doubt, Cuz, no doubt."

We hugged a little tighter this time and my ribs didn't even feel it. He did the same with Anjo, then made a point of telling Teresa in Portuguese not to take any of my bullshit. She told him not to worry. With that, Bones climbed back on the Sweet St. Pete to finish prepping the boat for departure. We turned and headed back towards the elevator.

As we hit the Plaza Cayru, in the shade of the Modelo Market we saw Wanda Miranda with a tray of pastries. When she saw us, she smiled like she'd known all along we were going to show up.

"Oy, bom dia, minha gente. Como vai tudo?"

We all responded in kind. Teresa and Anjo knelt and kissed her hand as well, giving me a clue about what was expected, so I did the same. Wanda seemed pretty happy about it as she spoke to me.

"Oy, Mike Breza, you like Detective Santos now?"

"It's Delegado Santos and yes, I like him very much."

Her eyes sparkled at me.

"And your ribbon from Bonfim?"

I pulled it out of my pocket and showed it to her. This provoked another smile.

"Your wishes come true?"

I looked over at Teresa, whose half-smile made me forget my pain. I looked back at Wanda and nodded.

"Yeah, Wanda, I think they did."

"And the figa give you luck?"

"Feels like it did."

"So you go home now?"

I shook my head.

"No, I'm staying. Things look pretty good right now."

I looked over at Teresa.

"I may be here for a while."